time AFTER time

Dedication

This one's for Mum and Dad, who remember the way I dressed in the 80s – and love me anyway.

Other Books by Judi Curtin

The 'Alice & Megan' series

Alice Next Door
Alice Again
Don't Ask Alice
Alice in the Middle
Bonjour Alice
Alice & Megan Forever
Alice to the Rescue
Viva Alice!
Alice & Megan's Cookbook

The 'Eva' Series

Eva's Journey
Eva's Holiday
Leave it to Eva
Eva and the Hidden Diary
Only Eva

Other Books

See If I Care

Judi Curtin

time AFTER time

THE O'BRIEN PRESS
DUBLIN

First published 2016 by
The O'Brien Press Ltd,
12 Terenure Road East, Rathgar,
Dublin 6, D06 HD27 Ireland.
Tel: +353 1 4923333; Fax: +353 1 4922777
E-mail: books@obrien.ie.
Website: www.obrien.ie

ISBN: 978-1-84717-872-5

1 3 5 7 8 6 4 2
16 18 20 19 17

Cover and internal illustrations by Rachel Corcoran.
Printed and bound by Norhaven Paperback A/S, Denmark.

The paper in this book is produced using pulp from managed forests.

Chapter One

Beth has been my best friend forever.

You know what it's like when you have a very best friend. It's like she's the only one in the whole world who really, really gets you.

You know what she's thinking and she knows what you're thinking, even when no one has said a single word.

It's like she's a part of you, the better part, the part that doesn't get embarrassed over stupid stuff.

You want to spend all your time with your best friend. You want to have sleepovers every Saturday night. You wish she was always around, ready to listen to your secrets and laugh at your jokes — even when they're not the tiniest bit funny.

You wish your best friend could be your sister, so she could live in your house and you could be together

every moment of every day.

My advice? Be careful what you wish for.

* * *

My dad left four years ago when I was eight. One minute we were a normal boring family and the next minute everything changed. The day after his forty-second birthday, Dad turned into a hippy and set off for Africa 'to find himself'.

Mum went totally crazy when Dad left. She stayed in bed for a whole week, crying and eating crisps. When I got home from school, there was never anything to eat, even though the whole house smelled like there had been an explosion in a crisp factory. It wasn't funny.

I wanted to help Mum, but I was only a kid – what was I supposed to do? And anyway, I was sad too. Mum was so busy feeling sorry for herself, she often forgot that I was missing dad too. We'd both lost someone.

Sometimes I sat by Mum's bed and held her hand, but it didn't make any difference. The pile of empty crisp bags and gross soggy tissues just spread further and further across the floor, while I got more and more scared. They make movies about the kind of stuff that was happening in our house – sad, black-and-white movies that don't usually have happy endings.

* * *

Then one day, after weeks and weeks, I came home from school to find all the windows in the house wide open and lively music floating out. I felt like doing a dance of joy when I heard Mum's voice calling to me. 'Hi, darling. Dinner's nearly ready. I'm just doing a little bit of craft work.'

Mum had always liked making stuff, so I felt good as I walked into the kitchen. I didn't feel quite so good when I saw the boxes of Dad's super-precious foreign DVD collection scattered around the floor. I felt sick

when I saw that Mum had sliced up the DVDs and was stringing the pieces together to make some kind of weird shiny, rattly curtain.

'Isn't it beautiful?' she asked. 'I'm going to hang it in the living room when it's finished.'

'But Dad's DVDs! One day he's going to want them. What's he going to say when he comes back home and finds out that you've ...?'

'Oh, don't you worry about Dad. He's a hippy now, remember? He'd love this kind of thing. Now, would you mind bringing down his ties from his wardrobe? I've thought of a brilliant way to turn them into a tablecloth.'

My big mistake was thinking that Dad was going to come back.

* * *

My first Skype with Dad was really weird. It was so nice to see his face, I couldn't find the words to tell

him how mad I was with him.

'Why did you go?' I asked, trying not to cry. 'Why did you leave us?'

The screen was all fuzzy and jumpy, but I thought I could see tears in his eyes.

'I'm so, so sorry, Mollikins,' he said. 'Your mum and I had been struggling for a bit, and ...'

'But you could have fixed whatever was wrong. You didn't have to run away. Why did you have to be such a total wimp?'

'I know it was cowardly, but I couldn't think of anything else to do.'

'Why can't you just come back home? Why can't we just pretend that none of this ever happened?'

He didn't answer my question, and I knew that was a really bad sign.

'I know I've hurt you, Molly,' he said. 'But you have to understand, none of this is your fault. I love you as much as ever, and so does Mum. That's never going to change.'

He said lots more stuff like that and after he'd gone, I lay on my bed and cried for ages. When I got up an hour later, I felt a lot better, as if the black cloud over my head was starting to float away a tiny bit. Like I said, it was very strange.

After that Dad Skyped whenever he could. We didn't cry as much, and sometimes we actually laughed. Even when he was hundreds of miles away, Dad was still funny, and he told me hilarious stories about the weird and wonderful people he met on his travels.

After a bit, I noticed that lots of kids in my class had parents who didn't live together. Beth's mum died when she was a baby, so she just had her dad to live with, and one boy I knew had never even seen his dad. I'm not sure why, but knowing you're not the only one makes things seem better, like your life isn't as crazy as you thought it was.

As the weeks went by, things changed slowly. Life didn't exactly feel right, but it stopped feeling so weird, which is good, I guess.

* * *

When everything Dad ever owned had been chopped up or mangled or dumped, Mum slowly came to her senses and started to act normally again – or as normally as she had ever acted. For a while things were kind of OK, with the two of us just getting on with stuff.

And then Mum started to get friendly with Beth's dad, Jim, something NO ONE had seen coming.

At first Mum and Jim started to sit together when Beth and I were playing basketball matches, which was kind of nice, because seeing Mum sitting on her own always made me sad. Once or twice the four of us went for hot chocolate after the game. I liked that, because sometimes when it's just Mum and me, things can get a bit too intense. I liked the way Jim didn't talk down to Beth and me. He asked what we thought about stuff, and he listened to our answers like our

opinions really mattered. And I guess it was nice for Beth too, because she's always got on really well with my mum, and they laugh at the same kind of lame jokes that are totally not funny.

They were fun evenings.

Then one Friday, Beth sent me a text. *'Dad and I are coming to your place for dinner. How cool is that?'*

'Totally cool,' I replied, showing just how innocent I used to be.

* * *

The doorbell rang on the dot of seven. Beth and I hugged while Mum and Jim did this weird shuffle, like they couldn't make up their minds whether they should shake hands or do the double-cheek kissy thing grown-ups love so much. It was a bit awkward, but I blamed the fact that Jim was holding a lasagne and a bowl of salad, and my mum was carrying our best tablecloth and the flower arrangement she'd been

working on for the whole afternoon.

During dinner Beth and I chatted as usual, but when the two of us had our mouths full, normal conversation almost stopped. It's never a good sign when you start to notice the clatter of cutlery on plates, and the sound of radiators clicking on and off.

'That flower arrangement is like something from the Chelsea Flower Show, Charlotte,' said Beth's dad.

Three times!

'This is the nicest lasagne I've ever eaten, Jim.'

I'm not sure how many times Mum said this – by the fifth time I'd pretty much lost the will to live.

'Isn't it adorable how your mum and my dad are hanging out so you and I can spend more time together?' said Beth when the two of us went upstairs after dinner.

'Yeah, but I wish they weren't so awkward. I thought they'd never stop going on about the flowers and the lasagne. It was like the world final of the lame compliments competition.'

'Totally – and it was hard work filling all those long silences.'

'It's like we're the grown-ups, trying to get the little ones through their first play date,' I said.

I should never have joked about Mum and Jim and dates.

That was mistake number two.

* * *

Things pretty much snowballed from there.

Mum got her hair cut short, even though Dad had always loved her long hair.

Lots of Mum's sentences started with 'Jim says ...'

She started to wear lipstick again.

Mum went over to Beth's place and made curtains for their living room.

I lost count of the times Jim showed up at our place saying, 'I just happened to be passing so ...'

I lost count of the times he just happened to be

passing with a dish of lasagne in the back of his car.

I realised that I've never really liked lasagne.

There were no more awkward silences at the dinner table. Sometimes Beth and I had to fight to be heard, because all of a sudden, Mum and Jim had an awful lot to say to each other.

Beth and I tried not to make a big deal of all of this. When you pass an ambulance at the side of the road, you can lean out of your car window and stare, or you can look the other way. Beth and I went for the looking-the-other-way option.

Mistake number three.

Chapter Two

It was about three months after the first lasagne date. Beth and I were hanging out in my bedroom, listening to music, when we heard Mum calling from downstairs.

'Girls,' she said, 'can you come here, please? There's something Jim and I would like to discuss with you.'

'OMG!' Beth's hands were over her face, so I couldn't tell if it was a good OMG or a bad one.

'What?' I asked. 'What is it?'

'Dad's been acting weird all weekend. He's been smiling way more than usual, and this morning I heard him singing in the shower.'

'Your dad can sing?'

'Well, only if singing's supposed to make your ears bleed – but that's *so* not the point.'

'What is the point? What's any of this got to do

with you and me? Are they dragging us downstairs to ask us to donate our pocket money so your dad can have singing lessons?'

'Stop being an idiot for a second, and let me explain.'

'Please do.'

'I bet you any money Dad and Charlotte are going to take us on a skiing holiday this winter.'

'OMG, that's totally—! ... how do you know?'

'A ski brochure came in our letterbox the other day.'

'That doesn't mean anything. We got one too – I think everyone round here did.'

'Yeah, but Dad's been promising to take me skiing every year since I was about six.'

'That's what they call an empty promise – you should know by now that grown-ups are experts at that kind of thing. What makes you think your dad's empty promise is suddenly going to turn into ... whatever the opposite of an empty promise is?'

'It makes complete sense. Last year I heard Dad talking about it with my aunt. He said that he really

wanted to bring me skiing, but that he was afraid it would be a bit sad and lonely – the two of us surrounded by big happy families.'

'So you think ...?'

'I think the four of us are going to go together. You and I are besties, and nowadays Dad and Charlotte are besties too, so it would be perfect. We're going to have such a fab time.'

'OMG,' I said. 'A ski trip would be totally amazing. Let's go downstairs before they have a chance to change their minds.'

* * *

Mum and Jim were sitting at the dining room table. I didn't get why they looked so nervous. Did they think we wouldn't like the whole skiing idea?

Beth and I were grinning like mad things. I was wondering how soon we could start shopping for ski gear. I couldn't decide if I'd like a white ski jacket or

a black one. Maybe I could get white, and Beth could get black, and we could swap every day.

'Hi, girls,' said Jim as Beth and I sat down.

Then no one said anything for ages.

What was the problem?

Why couldn't they just go ahead and tell us?

'This is a little bit awkward,' said Mum in the end.

'And it might come as a surprise to you girls,' said Jim.

'But we hope you'll be happy about it,' said Mum.

I couldn't take any more.

'Of course we're going to be happy,' I said. 'We're totally delighted, aren't we, Beth?'

'You know already?' said Mum. 'How—?'

'We're not babies any more,' said Beth. 'We can figure stuff out on our own, you know.'

Now Mum and Jim looked all pleased and relaxed.

'Phew,' said Jim. 'I have to confess I wasn't sure how you two were going to take it.'

'Why wouldn't we be totally delighted?' asked Beth.

'What's not to like about going skiing with my very best friend?'

'We're totally up for it,' I said. 'We're ...'

I had lots more to say, but something about the looks on Mum and Jim's faces made me stop.

'Skiing?' said Jim in a weak voice. 'Who said anything about skiing?'

Now I felt like a bit of an idiot. I couldn't even remember why had Beth and I been so sure about the skiing trip?

'Oh,' said Beth. 'We're not going skiing? That's OK, I guess.'

'But we *are* going on a trip, right?' I said.

Jim's face was the colour of the cheap, scratchy toilet paper they use at my school.

'I suppose we could go on a trip,' said Mum, who looked ready to start crying. 'But that's not really what this is ...'

'What's going on?' I asked. 'What's all this about?'

'Jim and Beth are going to move in,' said Mum.

A small part of me understood what she was saying, but a big part of me didn't want to believe it.

'Move in where?' I asked, even though, in my heart, I already knew the answer.

'In here, with us,' said Mum.

I felt like I couldn't breathe – like someone had punched me really hard in the soft bit of my tummy.

One look at Beth's face told me this wasn't exactly the best news in the world to her either.

'Isn't it great?' said Jim with a big smile. 'The four of us have been spending so much time together and we all get on so well, don't we?'

Beth and I just stared at him, and his smile faded a small bit.

'Anyway,' he said, 'from now on the four of us are going to live together. We're all going to be one big ...'

I put my hands over my ears. There was no way I was hanging around to hear the last two words. I ran upstairs, lay on my bed and cried like a baby.

Chapter Three

After Beth and Jim left, Mum came and sat on my bed. She held my hand and patted my back and said sympathetic stuff.

It was a bit like when Dad left, except this time I was the one in bed, and there were no crisps.

'Nothing's going to happen overnight,' she said. 'Jim and I want to give you and Beth plenty of time to get used to the new arrangements.'

Like two lifetimes?

How was I supposed to get used to the idea of a whole other family coming to live in our house with us?

* * *

The next few weeks were very weird. My house is my safe place, where I go when things outside are annoy-

ing me, and I wasn't sure I wanted to share this safe place with anyone else – even Beth. But how could I explain that to her, when she had to leave her lovely home to come and live with me?

Like I said, it was very weird, and the weeks went quickly, and before I knew it, Jim and Beth were moving in.

Usually when Beth stays over, she sleeps in my bed, but Mum thought she should have her own room.

'Best if you give each other a bit of space,' she said.

'We had space already,' I said. 'We each had a whole house full of space.'

Mum gave a big long sigh. 'This is going to take some getting used to,' she said. 'But everything will be easier if you try to be nice.'

So I was nice. I helped Beth to carry her stuff into the room next to mine. Together we unpacked her clothes and her books and all her other things. Then we sat on the bed and said nothing for a bit. We'd already talked a lot about the move, but now that it

had actually happened, I couldn't think of a word to say.

'There's a really good movie on in a few minutes,' she said in the end. 'Can we go downstairs and watch TV?'

I shrugged. 'Why are you asking me? This is your house now. You can do whatever you like.'

She leaned over and hugged me. 'This is totally weird for you too, right?' she asked.

'Totally. No offence, Beth, but I wish none of this had ever happened. I'm glad that Mum and Jim are happy, but this ... this whole thing is ...'

'Yeah,' said Beth. 'It totally is.'

* * *

Late that night I took my battered, one-eared furry rabbit and went into Beth's room.

'Any room for Hippity and me?'

Without a word, Beth made room for us under the

duvet.

'What are you thinking about?' I said when the silence started to get to me.

'My mum,' she said. 'At times like this, I really, really wish I had a mum.'

'I know,' I said.

She pulled away from me.

'Actually you *don't* know,' she said. 'You have no idea. Even if you live to be a million years old, you're never going to understand what it's like to be me.'

I felt guilty. Beth hardly ever talks about her mum, and when she does, I get all embarrassed, and don't know what to say. Usually, I listen for a second, and then change the subject as fast as I can. (I know that's totally cowardly, but I can't help it.)

'You're right,' I whispered. 'I don't understand. I don't have the faintest idea what it must be like for you – but you can tell me if you like.'

'It's kind of hard to explain. It's the everyday things I miss the most – the stuff *you* don't even think about.

The way your mum kisses you before you go to bed. The way you lie on the couch and put your legs up on hers, like she's just another piece of the furniture. The way she strokes your cheek when you're sad.'

'I'm so sorry, Beth.'

'It's not your fault, but now that I'm going to see your mum every day, it'll be harder for me. She always tries to include me, and that's really nice of her, but it's not the same. Living here won't change anything. Your mum doesn't love me, not the way she loves you.'

I didn't argue. How could I, when I knew she was right? The reason I can shout and scream at my mum is that I know she'll forgive me every single time. In the end, I'm always going to be her little girl.

'I wish I'd had the chance to know my mum,' Beth said then. 'When I think of her, she's all vague and blurry, like I'm seeing her through a fogged-up window. I don't know what made her laugh, or what made her mad. I don't know what her favourite colour was.'

'You could ask your dad?'

'I do, all the time – but it never helps. Last week I asked him what her favourite food was, and he said chicken curry.'

'Gross,' I said. 'But at least you know.'

'That's the point, I have no clue. When I asked him a month earlier, he told me Mum's favourite food was shepherd's pie. Every time I ask, he gives me a different answer. I don't think he remembers for sure himself.'

'I'm sorry.'

'I know it's not Dad's fault, but I just wish things were different.'

'Me too,' I said, thinking of my dad, far away in the jungle, and my mum downstairs watching TV with Jim.

Beth yawned and suddenly I felt a bit awkward. This was her room now.

'Er … I can stay here for a bit, if you like,' I said. 'Or I could …'

'Thanks, Molly,' she said. 'But I think I need some time on my own.'

'You can have Hippity for the night if you want.'

I was half hoping she'd say no. I *never* sleep without Hippity. But she stretched out her arms and took my rabbit.

'Thanks,' she said. 'Goodnight.'

I hugged her and went back to my own cold bed. It was weird. My mum was downstairs and my best friend was sleeping next door, but I felt like the loneliest kid in the world.

* * *

I opened my eyes.

It was Sunday.

Sunday is pancake day.

So why could I smell rashers?

I started to run downstairs, and then I remembered it wasn't just Mum and me anymore and I ran back to

put on my dressing-gown.

When I got to the kitchen, Jim was standing at the cooker, looking totally ridiculous in Mum's flowery apron. Mum was sitting at the counter, reading a newspaper. There was a plate of rashers and sausages and tomatoes on the table, and not a sign of a pancake anywhere.

'What's going on?' I asked.

'Oh, hi, Molly,' said Mum. 'Are you up already?'

'Are you stating the obvious already?'

'Now, darling.'

Her voice was sweet like golden syrup, but she was giving me one of the scary looks she'd been practising since the day I was born.

'Jim got up early to cook breakfast for us all,' she said. 'Isn't that nice of him?'

'But what about ...?'

'Why don't I make pancakes at tea-time?' she said.

'But we never ...'

Jim looked up from the egg he was flipping. 'I'm

sorry,' he said. 'Am I trampling all over your traditions? I just wanted to surprise you both. I guess I should have asked first.'

'It's fine, Jim,' said Mum. 'We love rashers and sausages too, don't we, Molly?'

I wanted to argue, but that look of Mum's wasn't going away. In fairytales, that's the look that turns people into lizards or anteaters or something.

'Actually, I'm not hungry,' I said. 'I'm going back to bed for a bit.'

I met Beth on the stairs. I'd almost forgotten that she was in the house.

'Do I smell rashers?' she said. 'Yum.'

I didn't answer. I walked past her, went into my room and closed the door behind me.

* * *

Things were kind of up and down after that.

Don't get me wrong – Beth and I were still the very,

very best of friends. It was cool that every single night she slept in the bedroom next to mine. It was cool that I could raid her wardrobe without having to walk to the other side of town. It was cool that she could do my maths homework, and I could help her with her history. All the things we used to do before we lived together were still great. It was the things we DIDN'T do together before that were weird: it was *so* not cool that, every evening, the four of us sat around the kitchen table, like we were a proper family.

It wasn't cool that my dad only showed up once every week, as a jumpy Skype picture, with palm trees and monkeys in the background.

It was hard to expect me to laugh at Jim's pathetic, embarrassing dad jokes, when my dad *was* a pathetic embarrassing dad joke.

It wasn't cool that Beth's mum was like an invisible ghost in our house, always there, but hardly ever talked about.

It wasn't cool that Mum tried to be Beth's mum

too. (That drove Beth totally crazy. Even though she always got on really well with my mum, now that they were living together, it was like they were both trying to be different people – and it soooo wasn't working.)

I know it was mean and stupid, but I couldn't help feeling jealous when Mum was being extra-nice to Beth.

And then there was the worst thing of all. When I saw Mum and Jim holding hands and whispering, I thought I was going to puke or die or both.

Chapter Four

'It's going to be amazing, Molly,' said Beth. 'We have to go.'

'We do?'

'Of course we do. Lucy says the afternoon concerts in Memorial Park are the coolest ever.'

'You don't even like Lucy. Since when do you want to hang out with her?'

'Since I saw her totally hot brother. His band is playing tomorrow afternoon at three, and we've just *got* to be there.'

'But we've got basketball practice after school tomorrow.'

'Mr Judge is a total pushover these days.'

She was right about that. Actually most of our teachers were going easy on Beth and me. As soon as they heard about our new living arrangements, they'd

been extra-nice to us, like we might run off crying if they said 'Boo' to us. Still, I didn't like taking chances.

'But what if—?'

'You don't have to do anything. I'll tell Mr Judge that the two of us have to go home early because of a domestic crisis.'

'That won't even be a lie. If Mum finds out we've skipped basketball, there *will* be a domestic crisis. And she'll go crazy if she ever finds out that I went to town after school. You know she only lets me go to town when she's there to act like a police escort, marching next to me, just in case I accidentally have a bit of fun.'

'Yeah, I know what she's like – and the awful thing is, sometimes I think my dad's turning into her. Remember how he went crazy the other day, just because I forgot to text him to say that I'd be home a bit late?'

I giggled. 'He might have lost it a small bit. But you're right – now that Mum and your dad are living together, they seem to be picking up each other's worst habits. That *so* isn't good news for us. So maybe

34

we should forget all about—?'

'No way! Lucy says her brother and his friends might hang out with us for a bit after the concert.'

'But there won't be any time for hanging out. Mum expects us home at five.'

'Not tomorrow, she doesn't. I told her that I've made it to the final of a debating blitz, and that you're coming along to support me. And Dad's working late, so I didn't have to tell him anything. We're free until seven.'

I tried arguing for a bit, but I knew I was wasting my time. Beth never gives up easily, and when there's a hot guitar-playing guy involved, well, it was a done deal before I even opened my mouth.

* * *

You could say that the next day didn't start well.

I had a huge row with Mum because she wanted me to stack up the dishwasher before school. I admit I

might have shouted a little bit. Jim was in the kitchen and he looked embarrassed, but I was too mad to care. In the end I jumped up from the table and slammed my bowl into the dishwasher.

'I hate you, Mum!' I shouted. 'I totally, totally hate you!'

After I'd done a bit more shouting, Mum confiscated my phone and put it away in the cupboard.

'You can have it back when you learn to show me some respect,' she said.

Then she came over and put her hand on my shoulder, but I pulled away, like her touch was burning me.

'I'm sorry to hear that you hate me,' she said. 'But I will always love you, Molly.'

Where did she learn that stupid line?

Was she deliberately trying to annoy me?

I felt like thumping something, but then Beth shouted down from upstairs.

'Come on, Moll,' she said. 'We've got to get ready. Remember you've promised to help me pick out cool

clothes for the debating blitz.'

If she was trying to help, it was an epic fail.

'Oh yes, Molly,' said Mum. 'I've been meaning to ask you about that. How come you didn't enter the debating blitz? Why can't you push yourself a little bit more?'

That made me *really* mad. 'You're saying you want me to be more like Beth?'

'Now you're just being silly. You know perfectly well that's not what I'm saying. I just think ......'

I didn't care what she thought, but I knew if I kept arguing I'd end up being grounded for months, so I ran out of the room, slamming the door behind me.

* * *

Upstairs, Beth was sitting on her bed, trying to stuff her new ripped skinny jeans into the bottom of her schoolbag.

'What started it this time?' she asked, when I was

calm enough to speak in full sentences.

'Mum's being totally unreasonable. She's taken my phone again – for nothing.'

Beth raised one eyebrow. 'For nothing?'

I put my head down. 'Well, almost nothing. Just because I didn't stack the dishwasher the very exact second she told me to.'

'So you ignored her? That's not the biggest crime in the world.'

I hesitated. 'Weeeell, I didn't exactly ignore her.'

'So what exactly *did* you do?'

'I might have said something about her being a total psychotic loser clean-freak who needed to get herself a life.'

Beth giggled.

'When will you ever learn?' she asked, sounding like an old woman.

I started to feel angry again. 'You just don't get it, do you? Mum knows exactly how to drive me crazy – and it's almost like she does it deliberately. She knows the

exact buttons to press to turn me from an ordinary girl into a mad person who wants to kick and scream and throw things. Sometimes I think she enjoys our rows. Sometimes I think mothers are more trouble than they're—'

I stopped talking and put my hand over my mouth.

'Oh, Beth, I'm so sorry,' I said.

'That's OK.'

'It's my big mouth. I should know when to stop.'

I should know not to give out about mothers to my friend who doesn't have one.

I looked at the photograph that Beth keeps beside her bed. In it, Beth is a teeny, tiny baby all curled up in her mum's arms. Beth has a red, scrunched-up face and her mum has crazy, wild hair, and she looks tired, but she's smiling like she's just won millions in the lottery.

Beth has heaps of cool clothes and stuff, but that photograph is her most precious thing. (After her mum died, the camera with all the other pictures of

them together got lost.) If the house was burning down, I think Beth would save that photo before saving me. I don't blame her though – the day after the photo was taken, Beth's mum fell down the stairs and died. It's the saddest thing I've ever, ever heard. Sometimes I wonder how Beth manages to get on with her life when something so awful happened right at the beginning of it.

'I'm really, really sorry,' I said again, wishing I knew more words to explain what I felt. 'Have I told you before what a cute photo that is?'

Beth picked up the photo. 'Only about a million times – but that's OK. I think it's cute too. My mum looks so proud of me, and I can never figure out why. I was only a day old and I'd never done anything except drink milk and burp and poop. Sometimes I wish ......'

'What?'

'Well, I wish Mum could know about all the things I've learned since then – like walking and talking and swimming and stuff. I wish she could know that I

managed to grow up, that I sort of turned out OK, that's all.'

'I bet she'd be really proud of you.'

'Thanks, Moll. It's just that Mum missed all of my childhood, and she's going to miss all my teenage years too. She's missing everything – and so am I. I'll never know what my mum was like when she was a teen-ager. I'll never know if she was cool or funny or weird or anything. It's like she's a total mystery – a mystery I'm never going to solve.'

I hugged her. 'I'm so sorry,' I said. Again.

Beth pulled away and smiled at me.

'It's OK, honest. Now go and pack your stuff for the concert. You don't want to be the only loser in a school uniform, do you?'

* * *

Mum was cleaning the oven when we got downstairs.

'I'm sorry, Mum,' I muttered. 'I shouldn't have said

all that stuff. I don't really hate you.'

Mum hugged me, and I didn't dare to pull away – even though she stank of old rasher grease and oven cleaner.

She gave a big sigh. 'That's OK, Molly. It's just that I was brought up to respect my mother, and I expect the same from you. It's not all that much to ask, is it?'

'But you were twelve once.' I resisted the urge to add – *a thousand years ago*. 'Are you telling me you never once lost your temper and shouted at your mother?'

Mum thought for a minute and then put on her primmest look. 'I'm sure I'd remember if I did.'

I didn't argue. There was no point – and besides, I wanted my phone back.

'So you were the perfect teenager?'

Mum didn't deny it.

'I loved being a teenager,' she said. 'It was a perfect time. We had long, happy summers. I used to steal your aunt Mary's Smitty and—'

'What's Smitty?' I didn't care, but listening to this ancient history stuff was probably part of my punishment.

Mum gave a big sigh. 'Smitty was the best perfume ever made. Mary always had a bottle hidden away and I used it whenever I dared – but then something awful happened.'

'You realized that it smelled gross?'

'No, smartypants. They stopped making it. Oh, how I'd love to smell Smitty again. It would take me right back to those happy days. It would ...'

I knew from past experience that Mum's reminiscences could go on forever, and I'd already heard way more than I needed. So I risked another dose of oven cleaner fumes and hugged her again.

It worked. She took my phone out of the cupboard and handed it to me.

'Just be respectful,' she said.

Then she hugged Beth too, which made me kind of sad.

How could Beth live without ever getting hugs from her own mum?

Did every hug from *my* mum remind her of what

she was missing?

'Good luck in the debating blitz,' said Mum. 'Would you like me to come along and watch?'

Beth smiled sweetly at her. 'That's so kind of you, Charlotte,' she said, 'but the hall is going to be full. I'll tell you all about it when I get home, OK?

Then Mum hugged us both again and we set off for school.

Chapter Five

After school Beth and I went into the toilest and changed into our proper clothes and shoved our uniforms into our schoolbags.

'I'm scared,' I said. 'Mum has this weird radar thing going on, and she always seems to catch me when I'm doing something I'm not supposed to.'

'You're just too nervous.'

'There's no such thing as too nervous where Mum's concerned. I wish we really were going to a debating blitz. What is that anyway? It sounds like fun.'

'There's no such thing as a debating blitz. I just invented it. Now hurry up, Lucy will be waiting.'

When we got to town, I started to relax a bit. Beth's excitement was contagious, and I was looking forward to seeing the concert.

'This is really kind of—' I was saying, when Beth

interrupted.

'Quick,' she hissed. 'We've got to hide.'

Before I could answer, she grabbed my arm, dragged me into an alleyway and pushed me behind a stinky, dirty skip.

'Hey!' I said. 'What's that about? I don't think Lucy's supercool brother will like you if you smell like a dustbin.'

'Shhhh. She'll hear you.'

I still didn't get it. 'Who'll hear us? Lucy? Why are we hiding on her?'

Now Beth clamped her hand over my mouth. 'Not Lucy, you idiot,' she whispered. 'It's your mum.'

I felt sick. If Mum caught us, I'd be grounded for weeks. Beth and I peeped out from behind the skip, and, a second later, Mum appeared. I didn't dare to breathe as she walked slowly past the entrance to the alleyway. Then, without warning, she stopped.

'What's she doing?' asked Beth. 'Why has she stopped? It's like she can smell us or something.'

'I wouldn't be surprised. We're dead, Beth. Totally dead.'

Then someone else appeared from the other direction, and I understood why Mum had stopped.

'Dora!' I heard Mum say. 'How nice to see you.'

I groaned.

'Who's Dora?' whispered Beth. 'And why are you making that awful noise?'

'She's Mum's third cousin or something. She's a nice lady, but she talks and talks and talks. We could be here for hours.'

Dora's voice floated along the alleyway.

'I haven't seen you in *ages*, Charlotte,' she said. 'I have *so* much to tell you, I don't even know where to start. But before I begin, what about you – has anything exciting happened in your life since I saw you last?'

I groaned again. 'No offence, Beth, but if Mum starts spouting romantic stuff about your dad, I think I'm going to throw up.'

'And you think I like to hear that kind of thing?'

She was right. All this was waaay too gross and awkward for the two of us.

Dora put down her shopping bags, like she was planning to be there for a very, very long time.

I turned to look the other way. The end of the alley was blocked by a huge high wall with barbed wire on the top. If this was a spy movie, we'd probably be able to make a ladder out of a few planks and wires that just happened to be lying around, and we'd be over the wall in seconds. But this wasn't a movie, and we were just ordinary kids. There was no escape.

'This is a disaster,' said Beth. 'The concert starts in a few minutes, and it could be all over by the time we get out of here.'

I hugged her – mostly because I hoped it would make me feel better. I don't like getting into trouble, and I don't like confined spaces, and the smell from the skip was totally gross.

'Hey,' said Beth, pulling away from me, 'what's that place?'

She was pointing at a small and poky looking shop with dusty windows and paint peeling off the door. Over the window was a faded sign – 'Rico's Store'. I wondered why I hadn't noticed it when we first ran into the alleyway.

'Let's go in,' said Beth. 'It's our only hope.'

'If they don't sell invisibility cloaks, I don't see how going in there is going to help.'

Beth rolled her eyes. 'Know what, Molly? The trouble with you is you've got no imagination. There could be a back door out of the shop – a way out of here without your mum seeing us.'

That didn't seem very likely, but I looked at Mum again and knew we had to do something. She was leaning against the wall of the alleyway with her arms folded and the look of someone who had no plans to go anwhere anytime soon.

'OK,' I said. 'You win – it doesn't look like we've got anything to lose.'

The two of us edged along the side of the skip and

stood in front of the shop.

'I'm not sure I like this place,' I whispered. 'It looks kind of scary.'

'Scarier than your mum?'

I shook my head. 'Actually, no.'

Beth took a deep breath, then pushed the door. It opened suddenly, and the two of us stumbled inside. Over our heads a bell jangled madly, then the door closed behind us.

I grabbed Beth's arm and squeezed it tight. As my eyes got used to the dim light, I could see that the walls of the shop were lined with rows and rows of crooked shelves. Each shelf was stacked with small, brightly coloured glass bottles.

'This place is so weird,' I whispered.

'Pardon?'

The voice came from behind me, making me jump.

I turned around to see a man – a very ordinary-looking man, wearing a suit and a white shirt and a tie. He looked like he should be working in a bank or an

accountant's office or something. He had a silver cloth in his hand and was using it to polish a sparkly blue glass bottle.

'I didn't quite catch what you said – maybe you could repeat it for me?' He sounded interested rather than angry, but still I couldn't help feeling afraid.

'Oh,' I said, hoping he couldn't guess how scared I was, 'I was just telling my friend that ... I feel a bit weird. I think I might have eaten something dodgy for lunch.'

The man looked at me, like he knew I was lying. (Even though I'm usually a pretty convincing liar.) I tried to look away, but something made me want to keep staring at his face. Then I noticed his eyes. They were bright, bright green, with golden flecks. Even though the shop was so dark, I could see them perfectly, like there was a light behind them or something. The man smiled, but it wasn't the kind of smile that makes you feel better.

I was starting to think that maybe I'd prefer to be

outside, hiding behind the stinky skip. I really, really wanted to run away, but the man was standing between us and the door – and besides, Mum was probably still lurking at the end of the alleyway.

He spoke again. 'As you may have guessed, my name is Rico, and it is a pleasure to make your acquaintance.'

The feeling *so* wasn't mutual, but I decided not to mention that.

'Er ... hi,' said Beth, sounding as scared as I felt.

'How can I help you two girls?' he asked.

'Er ... it's OK, thanks,' I said. 'We're good. We don't actually want anything.'

Now Rico leaned closer, and the gold flecks in his eyes flickered.

'That's perfectly ridiculous,' he said. 'Of course you want something. *Everyone* wants something.'

'Honestly,' I said, pointing at the rows of glass bottles, 'these are totally lovely and everything, but we're fine. We really don't want anything at all.'

'Not everything you want can be bought,' said Rico.

'Actually, there *is* something we want,' said Beth suddenly. 'There's someone outside that we don't want to meet. I can't explain why – it's kind of complicated, but we want to get away from here without her seeing us. Is there another way out of here?'

'So you *do* want something,' said the man, looking intently into Beth's eyes. 'And luckily, I can help.'

He waved towards a black velvet curtain at the back of the shop. 'The other exit is through there. If you leave that way, no one will see you. Trust me, it will be almost as if you were never here.'

Something about his words was making me nervous, but Beth didn't seem to notice anything unusual.

'Come on, Moll,' she said. 'We're out of here.'

Rico was smiling, showing us his perfect white teeth, which almost glowed in the dark. 'Go through the curtain and keep on walking,' he said. 'The door will take you to the other side.'

The other side of what? I wondered, but Beth had already vanished through the curtain, and there was

no way I was staying in that creepy shop on my own. So I muttered a quick thanks and pushed through the curtain after my friend.

* * *

Behind the curtain, it was dark – completely dark, like no single ray of sunshine had ever managed to sneak inside. The air was thick and warm, and there was a strong smell of cinnamon. There was no sound.

Something soft brushed against my face.

'Beth?' I said, trying not to panic.

'It's OK.' Her voice was muffled, like she was under-water, or far away.

'It's not OK. This place is way too scary for me. Let's go back. I don't care if Mum sees us. I don't care if she grounds me forever. I just want to get out of here.'

Something touched my arm and I gave a little squeal.

'Shhh,' said Beth. 'It's only me. Grab my hand.'

I did what she said, and the touch of her warm skin made me feel a tiny, tiny bit better.

'Rico was right,' she said. 'The door is just here. Hang on a sec while I find the handle.'

'Got it,' she said a second later. 'We're all sorted.'

I heard the click of a door handle, and then there was a flash of light, like we were famous and a thousand photographers were taking a picture of us. We stepped through the door, and it closed softly behind us.

Chapter Six

'Omigod, what's that awful noise?'

'What noise?'

'Can't you hear it? It's awful. Listen.'

I couldn't make out all the words, but it was weird stuff about pushing pineapples and trees and coffee.

It was a song.

A very bad song.

Probably the worst song I'd ever heard.

'Is that Lucy's brother's band?' I said. 'Please don't tell me we went through all that trauma to listen to this.'

Beth rolled her eyes. '*Of course* that's not Lucy's brother's band. Did I mention that they're actually good? The music seems to be coming from over there.'

My eyes were slowly recovering from the bright light, so when I turned my head, I could see the huge

speaker that was vibrating in time to the awful music.

'I don't get it.'

'They're probably just playing this weird stuff while the band's getting ready,' said Beth. 'It might be a trick, so after hearing this, we'll think Lucy's brother's band is really good.'

Suddenly I felt weak, like I was going to faint. I sat down quickly on a squashy pink couch and as soon as the dizziness passed, I looked around properly.

We were surrounded by huge leafy green plants.

It was like we were in a jungle – but what kind of jungle has big squashy couches?

What kind of jungle has huge speakers blaring out bad songs about pineapples?

What kind of jungle suddenly appears in the middle of a not-very-big town you've known all your life?

This was totally weird and scary.

It was like Beth and I had walked out of Rico's shop and stumbled into a whole new world.

'Where are we?' I whispered. 'I've never been here

before. I've never been *anywhere* like this before.'

'Be careful,' I said as she took a step forwards. 'There could be anything out there – tigers, lions, polar bears – anything.'

'How could there be …?' she began, but she didn't finish her question. She took another step, but this time she moved more cautiously.

I tried to stay calm, but I *so* didn't want to see what was on the other side of those plants.

Beth reached out and parted the branches.

'What can you see?' I whispered, not sure that I wanted to hear the answer.

'People,' she whispered back. 'I can see lots of people.'

'What kind of people? Do they look friendly? Do they look like the kind of people who … eat people? Do they look hungry? Do you think that song might be some kind of tribal war dance song?'

She shook her head. 'I don't think so. And no one's dancing anyway.'

'So what are they doing?'

She took another step forwards. 'I think they're shopping.'

I jumped up and pushed into the plant next to her. I breathed a huge big sigh of relief. Everything was OK. We hadn't managed to wander into a jungle. We were in the corner of a very big shopping centre.

We stepped around the plants and into the open.

'Phew,' I said. 'I feel like an idiot now, but I was really scared back there. That freaky shop made me crazy for a minute and I had no idea where we were.'

'So where are we?'

'We're in a shopping centre.'

'But *what* shopping centre? We're teenagers – we know every shopping centre for miles around. Think about it, Moll. A second ago we were in an alleyway off Main Street, and now we're in a weird shopping centre neither of us has ever seen before.'

'You're making me feel scared again,' I said. 'I don't like this place – something about it isn't right. Maybe we should go back? Mum's probably gone by now, and

it'll be safe again.'

I knew Beth was worried too because for once in her life she didn't argue with me.

'Sounds like a plan,' she said, as I followed her back through the plants. 'Let's hurry so we don't miss the concert. Wait till we tell Lucy about this place. Maybe we could all come here together after ...'

I bumped into her as she suddenly stopped walking.

'Hey!' I said. 'Watch it!'

'It's gone.'

'What's gone?'

'The door to Rico's shop.'

'A door can't just go.'

'So where is it?'

I pushed past her and looked. The jungly plants were still there. The squashy pink couch was still there (still with the print of my bum on it), but behind the couch there was just a plain white wall.

'See?' said Beth. 'It's gone.'

I didn't want to believe her. How could a door just

vanish?

'This can't be the right place,' I said. 'That crazy music wrecked our heads and now we're all mixed up.'

But no matter how far we walked in both directions, there was no door.

'Let's forget about the door into that stupid shop,' said Beth. 'I don't want to face that weird Rico guy again anyway. Let's just find another way out.'

Beth took out her phone as I followed her out of the jungly area and along the mall.

'I'll just call Lucy and tell her to wait for us,' she said. 'Hopefully we won't miss too much of the concert.'

But after a second she put her phone back in her pocket. 'My stupid phone's not working,' she said. 'I'm definitely going to ask Dad to get me a new one. Will you call Lucy instead?'

But when I took out my phone and clicked on Lucy's name, all I could hear was a series of loud beeps.

I shook the phone and tried again, but the same

thing happened.

This was too weird.

How come both our phones stopped working at the exact same time?

I was doing my best not to get freaked out, but it wasn't easy.

Two kids walking past were staring and pointing at me.

'What?' said Beth. 'Have you never seen a phone before?'

They laughed like that was hilarious, and then walked on.

'I *really* don't like this place,' I said.

'Me neither – and there's one thing I need to ask you.'

'What?'

'Why do you think everyone around here is dressed like the people in your mum's old photo albums?'

'Maybe we've wandered into the biggest fancy-dress party ever. It might be some kind of festival we've never heard about. That would explain a lot – and it

would be kind of cool too. We could ...'

'Look out that window,' she said, pointing. 'Why do you think all the cars out there look like they should be in museums?'

'You're just creeping me out,' I said, not wanting to admit that she was right.

Then I spotted a kind-looking woman walking past. 'Excuse me,' I said. 'What's this shopping centre called and how do you get out of here?'

The woman smiled at me. 'You poor little things,' she said. 'Are you lost?'

'Totally,' I said.

'Well, you're in the new Springfield Shopping Centre, and I agree it *is* a bit confusing at first. If you keep walking straight you can get onto Main Street, or if you go back the other way, you'll find an exit onto Robert Street.'

I thanked her and turned back to Beth. 'So this place is new,' I said. 'That's why we've never been here before – but I can't figure out how come we've never

even heard of it. Do you think maybe Mum was keeping it a secret from us in case we'd want to go on a mad shopping spree?'

Beth didn't answer.

'Anyway,' I said, 'we should probably go out the Robert Street exit, because that's closest to Memorial Park. And we should hurry, or Lucy will think we're not coming after all.'

I started to walk, but Beth didn't follow me. When I turned back, I noticed that her face was pale, and she was shaking.

'What?' I said. 'What's wrong, Beth?'

'I've heard of Springfield Shopping Centre before.'

'And you never told me? That's totally mean. Are you and Mum ganging up on me now? That's so not fair. I know Mum thinks you're great because of your fake debating blitz thing, but that doesn't mean—'

'Dad told me about this place. He made it sound like the coolest place ever. He and his friends hung out here all the time when he was young. It's where he

first met my mum. But ...'

'But what?'

She shook her head, like it was an etch-a-sketch, and she was trying to make her thoughts disappear. 'No. It's way too freaky.'

'*What?*'

'Dad told me the whole Springfield Shopping Centre burned down ... more than twenty years ago.'

'But that doesn't make any sense. If it burned down more than twenty years ago, how come we're here? Did they rebuild it? How did they do that without us noticing?'

Beth shook her head. 'They never rebuilt it. Some people died in the fire, so they decided they would never put another building on this site. Instead they turned the whole place into a park.'

'Memorial Park?' I said, waiting for her to laugh at me.

But Beth didn't laugh.

Instead of answering, she ran over to a newsagents.

I followed her and watched as she picked up a newspaper. When she looked at the front page, her face
went even paler than before.

'Break it to me gently,' I said.

'Is there a gentle way to say that it's Thursday the
26th of July 1984?'

Chapter Seven

Half an hour later, Beth and I were back sitting on the squashy couches. I felt all weird and dizzy, like I'd just been on the fastest, scariest rollercoaster in the world. We'd talked and talked, and still the whole thing didn't make any sense. Time travel *doesn't* make sense. Outside of books and movies, it has to be impossible.

But how else could we explain the fact that Beth and I had tumbled backwards out of our real lives and ended up in the 1980s?

In the end, Beth jumped up. 'Talking isn't going to change anything,' she said, 'and this music is doing my head in. We've got to get out there.'

'Out where?'

She waved her hands towards the plants. 'Out there. Out to the big bad 1984 world.'

'And do what?'

'Well, I'm not sure. I guess we'll have to figure it out as we go along.'

She pushed her way through the plants and walked out like she knew where she was going.

And I followed her.

What else was I supposed to do?

* * *

Nobody paid us any attention as we walked along. The loud music continued, with lots of bouncy pop songs that I'd never heard before, and hoped never to hear again.

'Hey, I know this one,' I said, when 'Dancing in the Dark' started up.

'How come?'

'It's ... it's my dad's favourite,' I said, suddenly feeling sad.

I wondered what was Dad thinking, back in 1984.

Did he have any idea that one day he was going to have a daughter, and that when she was eight he was going to abandon her so he could go off and live like a hippy?

'Sorry,' said Beth, giving me a quick hug.

'That's OK. I like hearing it – it doesn't make my ears hurt like the other songs did.'

'My eyes are sore too. Have you noticed that *everyone* around here is having a bad hair day?'

A woman walked past with wild, frizzy hair that made her head look like it was the size of my mum's pilates ball.

'Looks like hair-straighteners haven't been invented yet,' I said.

'I guess big hair is fashionable,' said Beth. 'Now ... or then ... or ... well in 1984.'

'Maybe. But if I ever end up looking like that, you've got to promise to shoot me, OK?'

Beth rolled her eyes. 'I'm glad you brought your sense of humour along. But we're trapped in the past,

remember, and I'm guessing that hairstyles might not turn out to be our biggest problem. Now let's go find a way out of here.'

We looked in the shop windows as we searched for the way out of the shopping centre.

'How do people wear this stuff?' I said as we looked at a display of colourful baggy shirts. 'Don't tell me mirrors haven't been invented yet either.'

I tried not to stare at a boy who was wearing trousers that looked like they were made out of a very big, very colourful tablecloth. Then I was distracted by a woman with HUGE shoulder pads.

'OMG,' said Beth. 'Is she wearing that outfit for a bet?'

'Maybe she's going to play American football, and she's got the gear on under her jacket?'

'Ha! She's totally ...'

'What?'

'Look around for a second, Molly.'

'At what?'

'I think everyone's staring at *us*.'

'But that's stupid. We're not the weird ones around here. These are my best jeans and ...'

But then I saw that Beth was right. They were being fairly polite about it, but everyone who walked past was looking a little bit too long at our clothes and our shoes and our hair. A few kids stared at our ripped jeans and laughed when they thought we weren't looking.

Maybe we weren't as cool as we thought we were.

* * *

At last we got to the exit of the shopping centre. We stood for a minute in front of the huge revolving door.

'Let's go home to see our house,' said Beth. 'That would be totally fun.'

'We can't go home,' I said. 'It's not built yet. What we know as home is probably still a wood or a field or a carpark or something.'

'How come you're so sure?'

'Mum has a totally embarrassing picture of me sitting on the front doorstep of our half-built house – and I'm wearing a nappy.'

'Gross. All this is scaring me a bit. I don't like the idea of being homeless. Do you think your granny's house has been built yet. That's near here, isn't it?'

I nodded. 'Yes – and Granny lives there now – in 1984 – too. She's often told me that she's been living in the same house for more than fifty years. She and Granddad moved in the day she got married.'

'Brilliant. Let's go see her.'

'That's a fantastic idea – not!'

'What's the problem?'

'What are we supposed to do when we get there? Do I go up to her and say, *Hi Granny, I know you're not all that old, but I'm your twelve-year-old granddaughter, and I'm not born yet, but that's only a small detail, and this is my friend, Beth, who hasn't been born yet either. Oh, and by the way, Beth's dad lives with my mum but*

I'm so not going into that right now and if you're not too busy, we'd like to hang out here for a bit while we figure out how to leap forwards in time to where we really belong? Could be just me, Beth, but I'm not sure that's a particularly good plan.'

'Very funny. And I'm guessing you've got a better idea?'

I didn't, but there was no way I was letting Beth know that.

'We could hang out here for a bit?'

'And do what?'

'It's a shopping centre – we could go shopping.'

'Do you see anything here that you'd actually want to buy?'

'Er ... no.'

'So, how about we go to your granny's house, and we can figure out what to do when we get there?'

'I guess. At least Granny's someone we know – being surrounded by all these freaky strangers is making me nervous.'

It wasn't a great plan.

It wasn't even a good plan.

But, since I couldn't think of a better one, like the characters in a totally weird fairytale, my friend and I set off for grandmother's house.

Chapter Eight

Usually the walk from Robert Street to my granny's place takes about ten minutes. There was nothing usual about the journey Beth and I took that day.

We walked through the door of the shopping centre and at first everything seemed fine. It was nice to be away from the jangly music, and out in the fresh, warm air. I had a sudden happy, adventurous feeling.

'This is kind of fun,' I said. 'Let's go around this way, past the ...'

I stopped.

'Past the what?' prompted Beth.

'Past the cinema – that doesn't seem to have been built yet.'

'It's 1984, remember. Everything's bound to be different to what we expect.'

I looked further along the road. 'After we go past the cinema that isn't a cinema, we can cross the road at the petrol station that ... looks like a field, and then we're supposed to turn left at the phone shop that looks a lot like a falling-down shed.'

Beth laughed. 'I'm completely lost,' she said, 'So let's hope your sense of direction is as good as your sense of humour.'

'Only one way to find out,' I said, and I led the way on the next step of our adventure.

* * *

We soon got used to the familiar-but-different land-marks, and the journey didn't seem so strange.

After a bit I took out my phone and looked at it.

'Still no signal,' I said. 'What about you?

Beth looked at her phone. 'Nope, none for me either. That's so ...'

'OMG, maybe mobile phones haven't been invented

yet?'

'Of course! Why didn't we think of that before? Dad's forever going on about how he and his friends managed to have a happy life without phones.'

'But how did they live? How did they manage, without being able to contact each other whenever they want?'

She rolled her eyes. 'I can't even begin to imagine.'

Just then we came to a corner. 'We're nearly at my granny's house,' I said. 'Do you remember it now?'

'Sort of. I've only been here a few times.'

'It's not far. Granny lives just around the corner. It's the first house, and it's always easy to see because of the huge trees all around it. When I was a little kid, Granddad built me a treehouse in one of them.'

'I don't remember a treehouse.'

'It blew down in a storm, and I cried for weeks about it.'

We turned the bend and I stopped suddenly.

'Isn't this it?' asked Beth.

I shook my head. 'No ... well ... I think it's the right place ... the house looks kind of the same ... but the trees are gone ... maybe ... I don't know.'

We walked a little bit closer, and Beth looked over the low brick wall.

'Are these the huge trees you were talking about?' she asked.

I leaned over the wall and looked at the scrawny saplings that were not quite as high as my knees. I looked more closely at the house. It seemed brighter and shinier than I expected. The front door, which had been blue for as long as I could remember, was bright red. But it was definitely my granny's house.

'I guess time changes everything,' I said. For a minute I felt sad. It was like someone had taken my darling worn-out Hippity and changed him back to the shiny new rabbit I'd got for my fourth birthday.

Beth put her arm around me. 'What do you want to do now?'

'I have no clue. You're the one who had the great

idea of coming here.'

'I suppose we could go in and ask your granny to help us,' suggested Beth.

'To get back to the future?'

'I guess.'

I shook my head. 'Sorry, Beth. My granny knows lots of useful things like how to knit and crochet, and how to get stains out of clothes, but I'm guessing she doesn't know a whole lot about time travel.'

'Yeah, but maybe she could—'

I'll never know what she was going to say next as she was interrupted by a sudden scream from the house.

'OMG!' said Beth. 'We should get help. Sounds like someone's being killed in there.'

There was another scream, and then the sound of an adult speaking in a slow, calm voice. Next came a big rush of very angry shouts. The shouts got louder and louder until at last we could make out the final few words: '… I HATE YOU! I HATE YOU! I HATE YOU!'

The calm adult spoke again. 'But I will always love you.'

I smiled. Where had I heard that before?

There was the sound of a door slamming, and then a girl appeared at the side of the house. She had huge frizzy hair, and she was wearing baggy yellow dungarees and a white shirt with a floppy collar the size of a small back garden. She stood there breathing deeply and looking like she wanted to punch someone or something.

'I think it's time to get out of here,' I whispered to Beth.

I was starting to back away when Beth grabbed my arm.

'Isn't that ...?'

'OMIGOD,' I whispered. 'It couldn't be – or could it?'

This was so weird. Long minutes passed, as I stood there like I'd been turned to stone. Then the girl saw us. She walked towards us with a fierce look on her

face.

'Is she going to recognise us?' asked Beth.

I shook my head. 'How could she? She's never seen us before. We're not born yet.'

'I'm glad I'm not born yet,' whispered Beth back. 'That girl is scaaary.'

That girl was closer now. I wanted to run away and hide, but it was like someone had superglued my feet to the ground.

'What do you think you're staring at?' she asked.

My mouth was hanging open (which is never a good look), but I didn't care.

My mum's eyes were staring at me from the face of a teenager.

My mum's voice was coming at me from lips that were very badly painted with revolting pale pink glittery lipstick.

My mum's chin had a huge, ugly red spot on it.

My fourteen-year-old mother was walking towards me.

This had to be the weirdest moment of my whole entire life.

How could this girl imagine that she was looking at her unborn daughter, and her daughter's best friend?

Did she have any idea that one day she was going to end up with grey hair and a saggy bottom that wiggles when she runs?

Would she shoot herself right then if she knew that one day she was going to have a twenty-minute conversation about which kind of washing-up liquid is the best?

Would she die if she knew that one day she'd be a woman whose idea of a fun day out is a trip to the garden centre?

She stopped in front of us and folded her arms. For a second, the only sound was the jingling of the tiny bells hanging from the ring on the finger where my mum's wedding ring should be.

'Well? Has the cat got your tongues?'

I looked at Beth for help, but she was doubled over,

and laughing like she was going to die.

'Beth, stop that,' I hissed. 'Control yourself and tell my ... I mean this girl, why we're here.'

Beth obediently straightened up and did her best to rearrange her face.

'Sorry about that,' she said. 'I just thought of something funny.'

My fourteen-year-old mother didn't look like she had a great sense of humour, but maybe we'd caught her at a bad moment.

'So why are you staring into our garden?' she asked. 'Trust me, there's *nothing* interesting here.'

Beth smiled her best smile. 'Sorry about that too,' she said. 'You see ... Molly and I ... we've lost our ... er ... our ... puppy, and we thought maybe he'd come in here.'

My mother smiled, looking a bit more like the mother I know and love.

'I adore puppies,' she said. 'I'll help you look for him if you like. Come on in.'

Beth looked at me and I looked at her, and then the two of us climbed over the wall and pretended to look for our non-existent puppy.

* * *

'My name is Charlotte,' said my mother.

She was holding her hand out and I didn't know if I was supposed to shake it or kiss it or what. (How was I supposed to know what 1984 kids did?) I held my hand out too and then felt like an idiot as I realised she'd just been admiring her ring. It was too late to pull away so we ended up doing this totally awkward floppy handshake thing. Her hand was warm, dry, soft – nothing like the hand I used to hold when I was a little girl.

'I'm Molly,' I said, 'and this is Beth.'

Suddenly Charlotte (I can't bring myself to call this young girl 'Mum') put her hand over her face.

'Oh no,' she said. 'How long have you been out here?

Did you ... hear me?'

Yes. And if I ever get back home, I'm going to give you a very hard time for pretending to be the perfect daughter who never ever did anything bad like shouting at her mother.

'No,' I said.

'Sort of,' said Beth.

Charlotte went red. 'This is very embarrassing,' she said. 'It's just that I'm so cross. My mother has announced that we have to go and stay with my aunt for the night.'

'Is that so bad?' I asked.

'It's a disaster. My boyfriend is on his way over, so the minute he arrives, I'm going to have to tell him that I can't go to a party with him like I promised.'

'Hypocrite,' I muttered, half under my breath.

'Pardon?' said Charlotte, whose hearing was clearly better when she was young.

'Oh, I was just thinking how lucky you are to have a boyfriend. My mum says I'm not allowed to go out

with boys until I'm sixteen.'

'She sounds a bit old-fashioned,' said Charlotte. 'Doesn't she know it's the 1980s?'

I started to laugh, but stopped when I had a very embarrassing thought.

'What's your boyfriend called?'

'Eddie.'

Beth suddenly collapsed into another fit of giggling.

I knew why she was laughing, but I couldn't join in. I'd always known that my mum and dad had been together for ages, but I had *no* idea that they were boyfriend and girlfriend when she was only fourteen.

Charlotte ignored Beth's laughing.

'He'll be here in a minute,' she said, 'so I can introduce you. He's a real hunk.'

'What's a hunk?' asked Beth through her tears of laughter.

'I can't believe you don't know what a hunk is,' said Charlotte, looking at Beth like she was crazy.

'You have to make allowances for my friend. She

used to live in America,' I said, like that explained
everything.

'Oh,' said Charlotte. 'Sorry. A hunk is a boy who's
very good-looking.'

'You mean he's hot?' I said.

'Well, I haven't seen him since yesterday so I don't
know if he's hot at the moment. Maybe if he's been
out jogging he might be a small bit warm.'

Now Beth looked like she was actually going to die.
I glared at her, and she did her best to recover.

'I sooo can't wait to meet your boyfriend,' said Beth,
reminding me that she's been a bit boy-crazy lately.
'He sounds cool.'

Charlotte looked confused. 'How could he be hot
and cool at the same time? That doesn't make any
sense.'

'And I'd really love to go to that party with you,' said
Beth.

'But you don't even know where it is, or who'll be
there,' said Charlotte.

'That doesn't matter,' I said. 'Beth suffers badly from FOMO.'

'FOMO?' said Charlotte.

I sighed. Being in 1984 was turning out to be exhausting. Who knew we'd have to translate so much?

'Fear Of Missing Out,' I explained. 'It's a popular saying where we come from. Anyway, thanks for your help, Charlotte, but I think our puppy has probably just gone home on his own. He does that sometimes.'

Then I pulled Beth by the arm. 'Come on,' I hissed. 'We're out of here.'

'But don't you want to meet Eddie?' asked Charlotte.

'Sounds good, but we really have to go,' I said. 'But I'm sure we'll meet him some time in the future.'

For once in her life, Beth didn't argue. We waved at our new friend, and then Beth followed me as I climbed over the low wall and set off around the corner.

'What was all that about?' said Beth. 'Can't we go

back for a while? I was having fun.'

'I know you were. *Way* too much fun.'

'I just wanted to meet your dad. That would have been so cool.'

'No, it wouldn't. It would have been totally gross. Dad's embarrassing enough as an adult. If I had to see him as a teenager, I think I'd throw up. And if you started chatting him up ... well that doesn't even bear thinking about.'

'Trust me – I would *never* try to chat your dad up, even if he was only a teenager.'

'Well, we'll never know, will we? Anyway, that's not the only reason I wanted to get away. If I saw my mum and dad all happy together, I might be kind of tempted to tell Mum how things were going to turn out.'

'What do you mean?'

'Well, should I tell her the truth? Should I say – *Eddie's going to grow up to be a really nice man, and you're going to have an amazing, beautiful, talented daughter, but when he's in his forties he's going to suddenly turn into*

a hippy and skip off to Africa, and you're going to go crazy for a while, and then my friend Beth's dad is going to start coming over and …?'

'Enough,' said Beth. 'I've heard enough. I think some things are better left unsaid. And anyway, if you told Charlotte all that, she might not marry your dad and then you wouldn't be born, and then … oh, this is really complicated, isn't it?

I nodded.

Beth suddenly looked serious. 'OK,' she said. 'You're right as usual. We won't go back to your mum's place. Let's go to …'

I didn't hear the end of her sentence, because she'd turned away and was already walking back towards the shopping centre.

I ran after her. 'I think I'll be able to find it,' she was saying, more to herself than to me.

'Find what?' I asked. 'Where are you going? You're not going to try looking for your dad, are you?'

'Of course not,' she said. 'Why would I want to find

my dad? I can see him any time I want.'

'So where ...?'

She turned and smiled at me with a smile that scared me a little bit.

'I'm going to find my mum.'

Chapter Nine

Beth walks very fast when she's keen to get somewhere, and soon I was exhausted from trying to keep up with her.

At last we came to a junction and she had to stop to let all the old-fashioned cars and bikes and lorries go past. I stood next to her, puffing and panting like I'd run a couple of marathons.

'Are you sure this is a good idea?' I asked as soon as I could speak.

'I want to see her.'

'I get that, but … a fourteen-year-old mum is … well … it's not normal. It's not right.'

'That's OK, then. My mum's not fourteen – she's thirteen, I've been working it out.'

'Whatever – it's not the way things are meant to be. You've got to trust me on this, Beth – I'm speaking

from experience. It was totally weird seeing my mum back there.'

Beth turned to stare at me. 'That is so, so different,' she said. 'You've seen your mum a million times, and when we get back to where we belong, you can see her again. You can see her every single day of your life.'

'Yeah, but—'

'If I ever want to see my mum, I have to do it now. It's my only chance. You just don't understand, Molly.'

At last she'd said something I totally agreed with. I couldn't even begin to imagine how she was feeling.

'I'm trying my best,' I said.

A huge, dreamy smile drifted across her face.

'Don't you see? I've got this amazing, precious, once-in-a-lifetime opportunity, and I have to take it.'

Suddenly I got a tiny glimpse of what it must be like to be Beth. I sometimes get mad at my dad for going off and leaving us, but I still get to see him and talk to him on Skype. I know that one day, he'll come back to visit and I'll get to hug him and laugh with him and

roll my eyes at his pathetic jokes. He's gone, but not forever. In lots of ways, I'm really, really lucky.

So what could I say?

This could all go terribly wrong.

This whole thing was going to be totally messy and weird and sad – but how could I come between my best friend and the one thing in the world that she really, really wanted?

'How do you even know where to go?' I asked.

'When Dad was driving me home from a basketball match a few months ago, he showed me the house where my mum used to live when she was a little girl.'

'And can you actually remember where it was?' I asked, half-hoping that she was going to say no.

'Sort of. Anyway Dad told me the name of the street, so I think we'll be able to find it – even without Google maps.'

'And when we get there? Have you thought about what we're going to do then?'

The traffic had stopped, and Beth was already half

way across the road.

'Let's just get there,' she called over her shoulder, and I had to run to keep up with her, as the traffic revved up to start moving again.

* * *

Much later, we were standing in front of a sunshiny yellow door. Beside us, bright pink and blue flowers tumbled down the sides of flowerpots. It was a pretty house, like something out of a fairytale, but a sick, scared feeling had wrapped itself around me, and I couldn't relax.

'Are you sure this is the right house?' I asked.

'Yes,' said Beth, 'I'm certain. Lots of things are different, but I remember the round window over the door.'

'I totally get what you're trying to do,' I said, 'but maybe we need to discuss it a bit more – before we do anything stupid.'

'No,' said Beth. 'No more talk. If I think about this, I mightn't be brave enough to do it ... and I *so* want to do it.'

'But ...'

Before I could finish, Beth knocked loudly on the door.

I really, really hoped that no one was home, but then I looked at Beth's excited face and felt totally mean. I held her hand and squeezed it tightly.

For a second there was silence, and then, from inside the house, I heard the sound of another door opening. Through the frosted glass panel, I could see a woman walking towards us.

Was I just about to witness the weirdest thing in the history of the world?

'It's my granny,' whispered Beth, letting go of my hand.

I've met Beth's granny loads of times – she lives in a retirement village not too far from our house. She's a nice lady, but she's old and grey and ... well ... she's

a granny. She walks with a stick, and when she sits down it takes her half an hour to stand up again.

The woman I could see through the glass panel of the door had golden blonde hair. She was wearing denims and a huge flowery shirt and she was practically skipping towards us.

I held on to the door frame, trying to stop my hands from shaking. I felt dizzy, like I'd stood up too quickly. I wished I was at basketball practice, or the dentist or basically anywhere else in the world.

The door opened and for a minute we all looked at each other. It was totally weird. Beth's granny came to our house for lunch last Saturday. She sat at our kitchen table for hours, telling us 'fun' stories about her active retirement group – and now she was acting like she'd never seen us before – like we were two randomers who'd just landed on her doorstep.

Then Beth's granny smiled. 'What can I do for you two girls?' she said.

'Is my ... I mean ... is ...?'

Poor Beth couldn't finish the sentence, and I knew I had to help her.

'We're looking for ... I began, but then it was like there was a huge lump in my throat, that was stopping the rest of my words from getting out.

Luckily Beth had recovered a bit. 'Fiona,' she said. 'Is Fiona home? We're friends of hers ... from school.'

Beth's granny smiled. 'I'm sorry, girls,' she said. 'Fiona is at her granny's house – in Kilkenny. She's staying there for another week.'

'Oh,' I said.

'Oh,' said Beth at the same time, like we'd been rehearsing it.

But how could we have rehearsed for such a bizarre situation?

'Thanks anyway,' said Beth in the saddest voice I had ever heard.

'When she gets back I'll tell her you called over,' said Beth's granny. 'What are your names?'

'Er, that's OK,' I said. 'Don't worry about it. We'll

tell her ourselves when we see her at school again.'

'Or maybe we'll call over again next week,' said Beth.

I stared at her, but she wouldn't meet my eyes. What could she possibly be thinking? How did she think we could live in this weird place for a whole week?

Where would we sleep?

What would we eat?

'Are you girls hungry, by any chance?' asked Beth's grandmother, like she could read my mind. 'I've just made sausage rolls, and my husband is working late, and I somehow managed to forget that Fiona isn't here to help me to eat them. They'll go bad if some-one doesn't help me out. Will I bring one out for each of you?'

Until then, I'd had too much on my mind to worry about food, but now that she mentioned it, I realised that I was very, very hungry.

And I suddenly became aware of the wonderful scent of warm food wafting from the back of the house.

And I remembered that, even in real life, where this woman is an ancient, creaky old granny, her sausage rolls are the yummiest ever.

'Yes, please,' I said, before she had time to change her mind. 'We haven't eaten in ... well, in a very long time.'

Beth's granny smiled. 'I'll be right back,' she said.

Beth and I ate the first two sausage rolls, and didn't argue when her granny went back for two more.

'Thank you so, so much,' I said, as I licked the last deliciously greasy crumbs from my fingers. 'You might just have saved our lives. Anyway, we should be getting out of here.'

I looked at Beth, but she didn't move. It was time to leave, so why was she hanging on, like there was something else she had to do?

'There's just one thing,' said Beth. 'Do you think you could give us Fiona's granny's address? We'd love to write to her, wouldn't we, Molly?'

Her words made me feel a small bit better. I didn't

love the whole letter idea, but if Beth was planning to write, that probably meant she'd abandoned any crazy ideas of hanging around waiting for Fiona to come back from her trip to the country.

'Wouldn't we love to write to Fiona?' repeated Beth, poking me hard right between my ribs.

'Oh, yes,' I said quickly. 'We'd totally love to. Our teacher says that letter-writing is a dying art, and that we should practise it at every opportunity.'

'That's ridiculous!' said Beth's granny. 'How on earth could letter-writing be a dying art?'

Because nowadays we text or FaceTime or WhatsApp.

'Oh, our teacher's a bit crazy,' I said. 'She's always saying stupid stuff.'

Beth's granny gave me a strange look. 'Let me get a pen,' she said.

Minutes later, Beth was holding a scrap of paper with an address on it.

'Thank you so much,' she said. 'Goodbye, Gr— I mean, just … goodbye.'

As soon as her granny had closed the door, Beth and I walked to a green area at the end of the road.

'Well, that was totally weird,' said Beth as she sat down on the grass. 'Who knew my granny was once so pretty, and so young?'

'But you must have seen photographs?'

'Heaps – but it's not the same. There's nothing quite like seeing your granny get thirty years younger over-night. Back there she looked like she could jog to America, but last week it took her twenty minutes to get from our living-room to the kitchen, and she had to stop for a rest on the way.'

Thinking about that made me sad, so I changed the subject.

'Are you really going to write to your mother?' I asked as I sat down beside Beth. 'That's kind of a cool idea, but where are you going to get paper and an envelope and a stamp? And what on earth are you going say to her?'

'I'm not actually going to write a letter.'

'Oh, good to know,' I said. 'Because that might have been a bit complicated.'

I felt better for one second, before I realised that something didn't make sense.

'If you're not writing a letter, how come you asked for the address?'

'Duh! Because we're going there, of course. We're going to visit my mum.'

Deep in my heart, I'd already known the answer, but when Beth actually said the words, I felt a sudden fear, like two cold hands were pressed around my heart, squeezing it tight.

It wasn't a nice feeling.

Chapter Ten

Wild and crazy dreams are all very well, but in real life, someone has to ask the hard questions.

'How exactly are we going to get to Kilkenny?' I said in the end.

Beth scratched her head and pretended to think. 'I know,' she said after a while. 'Why don't we walk there?'

'Walk?' I squeaked. 'But it's got to be a hundred kilometres or something mad like that – and you don't even like walking. Remember when your dad suggested doing that forest trail last week, and you faked a sprained ankle to get out of it?'

'I'm just kidding. We both know it's too far to walk. We'll get a train, of course.'

'Perfectly simple – except for one tiny detail. Have you got any money?'

Beth rooted in the pocket of her schoolbag and pulled out a few coins. She counted them out carefully. 'One euro and nineteen cents. What about you?'

I didn't need to check my pockets. I knew that I had exactly zero euros and zero cents.

'Wasn't stuff cheaper in the olden days?' I asked. 'Maybe we have enough for the train fare.'

'I doubt it,' said Beth. 'And anyway, I don't think they even have euros and cents in 1984. Whenever Dad talks about the Dark Ages, he mentions pounds and pennies.' She put the coins back into her schoolbag. 'This might as well be play money for all the good it is to us.'

'So we can't get the train to Kilkenny,' I said, trying not to sound too relieved.

'Sure we can. Come on, the station's this way.'

'So we're just going to get on a train with no money?' I said. 'How's that going to work?'

'We're clever girls,' she said. 'We'll make up a story.'

She marched off before I could even think of an

answer. Now I was starting to worry. Usually Beth's a reasonable girl who doesn't go much for crazy ideas – but suddenly it was like she was losing her mind, like she'd become a different person.

Of course I wanted my best friend to be happy – but I had no idea how it was all going to end.

***

We only got lost a few times on the way to the railway station. After a bit we got used to asking people for directions, instead of consulting our phones.

'She was really nice,' said Beth, when the second lady we asked walked around a corner with us to show us the road we needed to take.

'Yeah, she was,' I said. 'Everyone seems so happy to help us. Maybe Mum's right when she says some things were better in the olden days.'

'You know your mum will make you suffer if she ever hears you saying that, right?'

'Totally. This has to be our little secret. Now come on, or we'll never get there.'

* * *

'OMG,' said Beth when we got inside the station. 'This is like a set from an ancient movie. Any minute now Leonardo DiCaprio is going to show up to whisk me off into the sunset.'

'In your dreams,' I said, laughing.

Beth was right though, the train station was nothing like the one we knew. There were no ticket machines, and there were people in uniform everywhere. Passengers were wheeling luggage on big trolleys, and instead of lights, the information board had funny black flaps that clicked and rattled as they changed. It was all very strange.

'Perfect timing,' I said. 'There's a train to Kilkenny in fifteen minutes.'

'Platform three – my lucky number – that has to be

a good sign,' said Beth.

Beth and I went to platform three and peeped around a pillar at the ticket-collector who was tall and skinny and wearing an old-fashioned uniform. He looked mean – not exactly the kind of man who was likely to let us on the train without a ticket.

A few minutes ticked by. Part of me wanted to hang around doing nothing until the train left without us, but I knew that wasn't fair on Beth.

'I have a plan,' I said after a while.

When I'd told her, she didn't look convinced.

'No offence, Moll,' she said, 'but that's a pretty pathetic plan.'

'And you've got a better one?'

'Not exactly.'

'That's settled so.'

Two minutes before the train was due to leave, Beth and I picked up our schoolbags and rushed over to the ticket collector.

'Hello, er … Humphrey,' I said, reading the name

on his shiny badge. 'Our mum got on the train a few minutes ago. Her legs were sore after all the shopping she did, and she wanted to get us a good seat. She said she'd leave our tickets here with you.'

He glared at us. 'No tickets here.'

I gave a big fake sigh. 'Silly Mum,' I said. 'What is she like? She must have forgotten all about our tickets. I bet they're still in her purse. Will we go on to the train and look for her?'

Beth gave him her best smile, and, for one second, it almost looked like our plan was going to work. Then the ticket collector seemed to remember that he was a mean old man.

He stooped down so he was looking right into my eyes. 'Guess what?' he said.

'What?' I asked, trying not to sound scared.

'I don't believe you,' he said. 'I've been on this job for forty-one years and I know by now when someone's trying to pull a fast one.'

Beth actually grabbed his arm, showing me how

desperate she was.

'Please sir,' she said. 'You have to help us. It's a family crisis. We really, really need to get on this train.'

The man shook his head. 'Sorry, love.'

He didn't look the tiniest bit sorry.

'Pretty please?' I said.

'No can do,' he said. 'Unfortunately for you, I didn't come down in the last shower of rain. I don't believe your mother's on that train, and without a ticket you're not getting on it either.'

Just then there was a loud whistle and a burst of steam and the train began to move. The man closed the gate and locked it.

'Now be good girls and run along home to your mother.'

'Why don't you go home to your mother?' I said. 'Oh, wait – you can't – she's in a cage in the zoo.'

The ticket-collector shook his fist at us and said some rude words, and it seemed like a good time to get out of there.

'It wasn't the worst plan in the world,' said Beth, when we were safely outside.

'The only good plans are the ones that actually work. So that makes my plan a total disaster.'

She hugged me. 'Thanks for trying,' she said.

For a while neither of us said anything.

'I'm really sorry we didn't get on the train,' I said in the end. 'But maybe it's for the best. Maybe going to see your mum was a crazy idea after all?'

Beth shook her head. 'No way,' she said. 'I'm still going to see my mum – and maybe we should remember what your mum always says.'

I rolled my eyes. 'You shouldn't believe everything my mum says. She reads a lot of very dodgy stuff on the internet.'

Beth ignored me.

'If at first you don't succeed,' she said primly, 'you've got to try and try again.'

Chapter Eleven

For a long time we sat on the steps of the railway station, while people with big hair and weird clothes passed by.

We watched a woman carrying a huge suitcase through the carpark. By the time she got to the station door she looked like she was ready to lie down and die. The case didn't have any wheels, and I began to understand why the station was full of luggage trolleys.

'The wheel's already been around for thousands of years,' said Beth. 'How come no one's figured out how to put it on a suitcase?'

'Maybe they have – but if they haven't, we should tell somone. We could set up a factory and make a fortune.'

'I don't want to set up a factory and make a fortune,' said Beth. 'All I want to do is see my mum.'

I put my arm around her. 'We could try to get on a bus to Kilkenny?'

Beth shook her head. 'No point. Without a ticket, they won't let us on. We'd only be wasting our time.'

'Or we could hitchhike?'

It was a stupid suggestion, but I was running out of ideas. Luckily, Beth wasn't that desperate.

She shook her head again. 'Absolutely not,' she said. 'Hitchhiking's much too dangerous. There's no way I'm getting into a car with a stranger. And remember, no one has any idea where we are. If we went missing, no one would even know.'

That reminded me. I checked my watch. 'OMG!' I said. 'Who cares about Kilkenny? Look at the time. Mum's going to go crazy if I'm home late – and I can't even text her a made-up excuse. I'm so dead, Beth.'

Beth just smiled, which made me kind of mad.

'And I don't know what you think is so funny,' I said. 'Your dad's probably home by now too – and if Mum's mad, you know he's going to join in too. Face it, Beth,

we're both totally, totally dead. You might as well enjoy your time in 1984, because I don't think you and I are going to be allowed to go out for another thirty years.'

Beth was still smiling. 'Maybe we're not dead,' she said.

'How come?'

'Well, haven't you ever read about time travel?'

'Not a whole lot.'

'It's like there are rules.'

'What kind of rules?'

'Usually, no matter how much time passes, when the time traveller gets back home to their proper life, no time has passed at all.'

She kind of had a point, but I wasn't giving in that easily.

'That would be fine if we were in a book,' I said. 'But since this is real life, I'm not sure how it's going to help us. I think this adventure is over, Beth. We have to try to get home, before Mum and Jim call the police.'

I stood up. 'Come on,' I said. 'Let's go back to the

shopping centre. Maybe the door to Rico's weird shop will have magically reappeared. If we hurry, we might even catch the end of the concert.'

Beth didn't move, and for a second, I had a glimmer of what she had lost. 'I'm sorry,' I said. 'I'm sorry you didn't get to see your mum. It would have been really nice for you, but ...'

'You can do what you want, but I'm not going anywhere.'

'You've got to come with me. I can't go back into that shopping centre on my own. What if all those freaky-looking people decide to gang up on me? If a woman with giant shoulder pads tries to hug me, I could be smothered to death.'

Beth didn't even smile. 'You heard me. I'm not going with you.'

'But ...'

'I've made up my mind. Until I've seen my mum, I'm not going anywhere near that shopping centre or Rico's shop. I'm not going to waste this opportunity.'

'I get that you're disappointed, but your mum is miles and miles away, and we have no idea how to get to her. We've got no money and no food and nowhere to sleep. It's going to be dark soon, and—'

'Everything you're saying makes perfect sense, but I'm not changing my mind. It's getting late now, so I'm going to find somewhere to sleep, and in the morning, I'm going to find my mum – with or without you.'

For a second I remembered the way Rico stared at Beth. I heard his words again – so you *do* want something!

Was this some weird kind of fate?

But in the end it was the hint of tears in Beth's eyes that got to me.

'I guess if it's with or without me, then you'd better count me in,' I said.

'OMG! OMG! OMG! Thank you so, so much.'

She hugged me for a long time. I smiled when she finally pulled away. It's nice when you can help to make your best friend's dreams come true.

Nice but scary.

* * *

'Are you sure we can't go back to your granny's place for the night, Beth?' I was totally fed up after an hour of trailing around the strange but familiar streets of our town.

'Absolutely. We can't possibly explain to her who we are, and it's not fair to try – the poor woman could have a heart attack or something. But if you're that tired, maybe you'd like to try your mum's place?'

'Not in a million years. I'm still freaked out from that experience – and anyway, she's gone away for the night, remember?'

'How convenient.'

Beth was still walking, like she actually had a destination in mind.

'So where exactly are we going?' I asked. 'What's the plan? Please, Beth, tell me you've got a plan.'

'I've time-travelled a million times before – so I'm full of plans – not! This thing is new to me too, you know, Molly. All I'm thinking is that if we keep walking, in the end we'll find somewhere safe and warm to sleep.'

'Like where exactly? Do you think we're going to go round the next corner and see a five-star hotel with a big sign outside – NO CHARGE FOR TIME TRAVELLERS? We could get someone to massage our sore feet, and then we'll have dinner and a swim, before settling down for the night in a four–poster bed piled high with fat and squishy white pillows.'

'Very funny. Trust me, Moll. Let's just keep walking and I promise I'll find us somewhere to spend the night.'

And to be fair to her, in the end she did.

Chapter Twelve

'Look. It's a school.'

I found it hard to be enthusiastic. It was dark by now, and I was cold and hungry and more scared than ever. 'Oh, goody,' I said, 'a school. Maybe it'll be open, and we can go in and learn some long division or some history or—'

'It's night time. Of course it won't be ...'

Beth stopped talking, because as we came around a bend we could see that there were lights on in one of the classrooms. A group of women were sitting inside, watching another woman who was writing on a blackboard.

'We're in luck,' whispered Beth. 'It's a night class.'

'Brilliant,' I said. 'Why don't we go in and learn some Italian, or Greek or something like that. Maybe they're giving lessons on how to survive when you've

gone back in time and haven't got any money.'

'Shut up, Dorkhead. We're not going to go to the night class, but I bet the front door is open, so we can sneak in and hide until the class is over. Then we can find ourselves somewhere to sleep, and we're sorted.'

A warm place to sleep sounded very tempting, but this still sounded crazy.

'But ... but ... that's against the law. Isn't it?'

'I guess – but we're desperate.'

'So if you're desperate, the law doesn't matter?'

'We won't do any damage. We'll just go to sleep, and in the morning we'll leave the place exactly like we found it. What's wrong with that?'

She made it sound simple. There had to be a catch. Only trouble was, I was too tired to think of one.

It was too risky to walk up the driveway, so we climbed over a fence and went along a narrow path to the side of the building.

'Try the door and see if it's unlocked,' said Beth.

'Why me? This was all your idea in the first place.'

Beth didn't answer.

Suddenly I understood the seriousness of what we were doing. How had our lives gone in such a weird direction?

'Let's just think about this for a minute,' I said. 'We're normal kids. We do normal stuff like hanging out and playing basketball. We should be at home, eating pizza and fighting about what to watch on TV. We don't do things like breaking into schools, so we won't have to sleep in the street. What's going on here? What's happened to us?'

Still Beth didn't answer.

I looked closely at her. She looked young and lost – a bit like I was trying not to feel. I remembered how much this whole thing meant to her.

'You really, really want to see your mum, don't you?' I asked.

I thought she hadn't heard me, but then I saw that her eyes were full of tears, sparkling in the light from the hallway.

I took her hand and squeezed it tight.

'Come on,' I said. 'Let's get this over with.' I reached out, turned the handle, and pushed. Without even the faintest squeak, the door slipped open. We were in.

* * *

Inside the school, there was a corridor leading left and right. We could hear voices coming from the left, so we went the other way. We tiptoed along the corridor until we came to another door.

'Now what?' I asked.

Beth pushed the door open and we stepped through. We were in a big hall, with four doors leading off it. The streetlights made everything seem big and shadowy and scary.

'Now what?' I asked again.

'Now you learn to say something else besides, *Now what?*' said Beth.

'What now?' I suggested. We both started to giggle. It wasn't funny-giggling though. It was more like this-is-the-craziest-thing-we've-ever-done-and-we're-starting-to-feel-very-nervous-giggling.

Suddenly Beth was serious. 'Listen carefully, Molly,' she said. 'This is what we're going to do. We're going to open that door there.'

'Why that one?'

'Just because. We're going to go into the room, and we're going to wait there until the night class is over and everyone's gone home.'

I followed Beth as she pushed open the door nearest to us and stepped inside. I tripped over a tiny chair and cracked my knee on the hard, tiled floor.

'Ow,' I squealed.

'Shush. Do you want to spend the night in a police station?'

'Would it be warm and cosy, and would I get something to eat?'

'This isn't funny, Molly. This is real. If we get caught,

we're in serious trouble. Don't you understand?'

I nodded, which was a bit stupid because it was too dark for Beth to see.

Beth took my arm. 'Here's the wall. Feel your way along it, and find a space to sit down.'

'And then?'

'And then we wait.'

I don't usually like it when Beth bosses me around, but now I was kind of glad. It was nice, trusting her to be in charge.

It didn't take me long to find myself a clear patch of floor. I dropped my schoolbag and sat down beside it.

And then we waited.

And waited.

And waited.

After what felt like about three weeks, we heard the sound of a door opening, followed by voices and laughing. I hardly dared to breathe as multiple footsteps moved along the corridor, getting closer and closer. My heart was thumping like it wanted to jump

out of my chest and tap-dance around the room.

'What if they come in here?' I whispered in a panic.

'Then we're in a big pile of trouble.'

Suddenly I had a horrible thought.

'What if they switch on a burglar alarm? What if there's electronic beams that will set it off if we breathe or move our little fingers or something?'

'Nah,' said Beth. 'It's the 1980s, they didn't have alarms back then.'

'Are you certain?'

'Er ... sort of. I bet they didn't have motion sensors, anyway – but I guess we'll find out soon enough.'

There was the rattle of keys, the sound of a door closing, a chorus of goodbyes and then silence.

'I didn't hear any alarm beeping,' said Beth in the end. 'Did you?'

'No, but maybe it was just too far away.'

I stood up slowly, expecting to hear an alarm shrieking. I half-closed my eyes, ready to protect them from blinding lights. There was nothing though. All I could

see were shadows, and the only thing I could hear was the sound of Beth's breathing.

I waved one arm and then the other in the air, and still nothing happened. Beside me, I could feel Beth standing up too.

'Do you think it would be safe to put on the lights?' I asked.

'I don't think that's a good idea. What if someone outside sees them?'

'But you know the dark makes me nervous.'

I jumped as something touched my arm.

'Sorry,' said Beth. 'That was me. I was trying to hold your hand to make you feel better.'

She found my hand and squeezed it tight. It did make me feel better – for a second. But then the good feeling passed, and I was still stuck in a dark, locked-up school, far away from my home and family.

Just then my stomach made a loud rumbling noise, reminding me that it was hours and hours since Beth's granny had fed us those delicious sausage rolls.

'I need food,' I said. 'If I don't get something to eat soon, I don't think I'll make it through the night. And if I'm dead, I'm not going to be great company tomorrow.'

'Always the drama queen! But I'm kind of hungry myself. Let's go find something to eat.'

I held on to Beth's hand as she led the way through the dark school. Falling and breaking our necks wasn't really part of our plan, so we decided to risk using the light on Beth's phone.

I know schools aren't totally fun places anyway, but in the middle of the night, this one was really scary. The phone only lit up the tiniest patch in front of us, and everything else was dark and creepy. I couldn't see into the shadowy areas, and I kept thinking that something horrible was going to jump out and grab me. We spoke in whispers, even though I very, very much hoped that there was no one around to hear us.

'What are you looking for?' I asked as Beth closed what felt like the hundredth door.

'The staffroom.'

'That sounds like a good idea,' I said. 'We can sit inside and pretend to be teachers. We can talk for hours about maths and history and really hard home-work.'

'No, smartypants, we're not going to do that. We're going to raid the fridge. You know what teachers are like – always drinking tea and shoving food into their faces while we're made go outside in the freezing cold.'

'But it's July. They won't have left any food here.'

'Possibly. But let's hope the teachers here are care-less. Maybe they were so glad the holidays were here that they just ran home quickly, leaving the staffroom stuffed with food.'

She opened the next door and I followed her inside. She waved her phone around the room until the light landed on a large, white, shiny rectangle.

'Yesss!' I whispered, wondering when I'd last been so excited by the sight of a fridge.

My mouth was already watering as I raced over

and pulled the fridge open. Light poured out and I slammed it shut again.

'It's OK,' whispered Beth. 'We're at the back of the school now. No one will see us. Open it again and see what's inside.'

I did as she said, and then felt like crying. There was nothing in the fridge except a cold-pack for putting on bruises.

I closed the fridge and slumped down onto the floor next to it. 'I told you they wouldn't leave food here over the holidays,' I wailed. 'We're going to starve to death. The teachers will come back in September and find two skeletons lying in the middle of their precious staffroom. They'll probably use our bodies for their science lessons next year.'

Beth opened a cupboard. 'There are teabags,' she said. 'That's good. We could make ourselves a nice cup of tea.'

'What part of starving don't you understand? A cup of tea isn't going to save my life – especially if there

isn't any milk in it.'

'Wow, Molly, look over here.'

I found the energy to go over and look. On a counter in the corner of the room there was a big, round tin with a label – *Luxury Chocolate Biscuits*. It looked like the tin my granny uses for keeping old buttons and ribbons and stuff – except Granny's tin is all old and scratched, and this one was shiny and new.

We looked at the tin for ages. I was afraid to touch it, and I was guessing Beth felt the same.

'What if it's empty?' I said. 'If it's empty I think I'm going to die.'

'Enough already about dying,' said Beth, as she picked up the box. A slow smile spread across her face. 'It's heavy,' she said. 'Really heavy.'

I was still half afraid to hope. 'It might be full of pencils, or crayons or confiscated chewed chewing gum,' I said.

Beth shook her head. 'It's not. Look, Moll, the lid is sellotaped on. Our dreams have come true. We've

found a whole box of chocolate biscuits.'

I started to rip the sellotape off the tin, but Beth put her hand on mine and stopped me.

'This is stealing,' she said. 'And stealing is wrong.'

'Breaking into schools is wrong – and we've just done that, haven't we? Starving to death is wrong too. This is an emergency, Beth. Teachers are supposed to love kids, and if they knew they were saving our lives, they'd be happy to share their food with us.'

It was a good argument, and it worked. Beth ripped off the rest of the tape and opened the tin. The biscuits looked like the ones Mum buys at Christmas – except they were smaller, like they'd shrunk a bit. Beth held the tin towards me, and my hand shook as I grabbed two biscuits and shoved them into my mouth. They were the most delicious things I'd ever tasted in my whole life. When Beth had eaten two biscuits, she found the kettle, boiled it up and made a pot of tea. Then the two of us sat at the table in the staffroom of the dark and creepy school, and dunked luxury choc-

olate biscuits into our tea until we couldn't eat any more.

'Time for bed,' said Beth, when I yawned for the tenth time. 'But first we need to tidy up.'

I rolled my eyes, but still I helped her to wash and dry the cups, and put everything back into place.

'Perfect,' she said when we were finished. 'Just like we found it.'

'Except for the small detail of the half-empty box of biscuits.'

We went back to the hall and found a pile of lovely soft PE mats. We dragged some of them into a classroom and made a sort of bed. It was cold, so we found a rack of left-behind coats and put a few of them on.

'It's too dark to be certain,' said Beth, 'but I'm guessing we look like total idiots.'

I giggled. 'Look on the bright side. YouTube hasn't been invented yet. No one need ever know.'

We lay down on the mats. It was nice having Beth so close, but, even so, I couldn't help missing my mum

and wishing I could be near her. That was impossible though. My grown-up mum was far away and I had no idea how to get back to her. And what would my teenage mum say if I tracked her down and said I needed her to cuddle me and stroke my hair and rub circles on my back and tell me that she would love me forever? There are probably laws against that kind of thing.

During the night I had terrible nightmares. I kept dreaming that people were chasing us and trying to send us to jail. Once I cried out, and Beth reached over and held my hand. The next time I woke up we were cuddled up together, and Beth had her arms around me, like I was a baby.

After that I slept for a long time.

Chapter Thirteen

I opened my eyes, and wondered where I was.

Oh yes, my best friend and I had just spent the night on the floor of a school.

In the summer holidays.

In 1984.

Had to be a bad dream.

I closed my eyes and opened them again.

Still the same.

I was still wearing a raggy old parka belonging to someone with much shorter arms than me. Beth was still wearing an ugly jacket with a picture of Action Man on the back.

I was in the 1980s even though I wasn't going to be born for another twenty years.

Today we had to figure out how to get to Kilkenny to see Beth's mum, who was supposed to be a dead

grown-up, but was instead a very-much-alive thir-teen-year-old.

Beth opened her eyes. 'Is this a dream?'

I shook my head. 'Unfortunately not. This might be crazy and weird, but it *is* happening.'

'Oh, good. I was worried for a minute. Now get up, Moll. We've got a big day ahead of us.'

She was already on her feet and prowling around the classroom.

'This is one mean teacher,' she said after a while.

'Why?'

'Look.' She pointed at a chair labelled 'naughty chair'.

Then there was a dark corner with a big sign hang-ing over it – 'naughty corner'.

I looked at the blackboard. There was a heading 'naughty children', and underneath it the names of five boys and girls.

I jumped up, grabbed the blackboard cleaner and rubbed out the names. 'The poor things,' I said.

'Imagine having your name up there for the whole holidays.' I had a sudden brainwave. 'What's the teacher's name?'

I didn't wait for Beth to answer. I opened a drawer in the teacher's desk and pulled out a diary. 'Joan Leahy' it said inside the cover. I picked up the chalk and changed the heading on the blackboard to 'Very, very naughty children', and then I wrote the teacher's name in capital letters underneath it.

I rubbed the chalk off my hands and gave a big happy sigh. 'Revenge of the naughty children,' I said. 'Now isn't it time for breakfast?'

* * *

In daylight the school wasn't spooky any more. It just felt empty and sad and lonely – almost like it missed the noisy children who should be racing around the corridors and slamming the doors.

When we got back to the staffroom, Beth made tea,

I put some luxury chocolate biscuits on plates, and we settled down for our feast. When we were totally full, I found a bottle by the sink and filled it with water, then put what was left of the biscuits into a plastic bag.

'The teachers were probably saving these biscuits for a treat on their first day back to school in September,' said Beth. 'They're so not going to be happy when they see that there's only crumbs left.'

'Maybe they'll think the biscuits were eaten by very clever, very tidy mice.'

Suddenly I had an idea. I found a piece of paper and a pencil, and wrote a note. *Sorry everyone, I just couldn't resist – I can be a real pig sometimes!* I signed it Joan Leahy. Then I put it inside the biscuit box, replaced the lid, and put the box back where we found it.

'OMG, that's totally evil,' said Beth.

'I know. Great, isn't it? Now isn't it time we got out of here?'

We tidied up the staffroom again, and when we got back to the classroom, Beth hung the raggy coats back

on the lost-property rail.

'No one is ever going to claim these,' she said. 'I bet if we come back here in our real time, they'll still be here.'

'Even if this school still exists, I'm never coming back here. What if Joan Leahy catches me? She'll put me in the naughty corner for a hundred years.'

We dragged the PE mats back where we found them, packed up our biscuits and water, and quietly let ourselves out of the school, closing the door behind us.

When we were back on the street we stopped and looked at each other for a moment.

'How exactly are we going to get to Kilkenny?' I asked.

'I've been thinking about that, and I've got a plan. Just follow me.'

* * *

If I'd known that Beth's clever plan involved going back to the railway station, I'd have said no at once. I had zero desire to see Humphrey the evil ticket checker again. But Beth probably knew that, so she said nothing until we got there.

We'd just missed a train to Kilkenny, and the next one wasn't for ages and ages. We passed the time by having a biscuit picnic in the park.

'No offence, Beth,' I said, when we finally returned to the station. 'But what makes you think Humphrey's going to let us on the train today?'

She smiled. 'Today I've got a bigger and better plan. Just give me a sec.'

I watched as she switched on her phone and started to type.

'Here,' she said when she was finished. 'What do you think?'

I read the text on her screen, and had to admit it was pretty impressive.

EXPERIMENTAL ELECTRONIC BOOKING SYSTEM: 2 RETURN TICKETS TO KILKENNY 27 JULY 1984

* * *

'You two again! And where is your invisible mother today?' Humphrey hadn't got any nicer overnight.

Beth smiled sweetly. 'Oh, our mum's not here. Today it's just us two.'

'Let's see your tickets.'

She smiled again. 'Here they are.'

She held her phone towards him and he looked at it like it was a bomb that could go off at any second.

'I've never seen anything like this before,' he said. 'Is it some kind of new-fangled calculator or what?'

'It's an MBS,' said Beth. 'A Mobile Booking Console.'

Humphrey took a huge pair of glasses from his pocket and read the text on the screen.

'What kind of a joke is this?' he said.

'Oh it's not a joke at all,' I said. 'It's very serious. Haven't you heard about the new booking system? Didn't you get an e-mail ... I mean a letter or something?'

'It's the future – today,' added Beth. 'In twenty years time, everyone's going to have electronic tickets.'

Humphrey narrowed his eyes, but said nothing. It was nearly time for the train to leave, so I decided to bluff a bit more.

'Why don't you go and check, if you don't believe us?' I said. 'There's a very important-looking man in the booking office, and I'm sure he'd be really happy to help you – if he's not really mad at you for not knowing about the new system.'

Humphrey's mouth went all twisty and he looked like his brain was being torn in two. Clearly he only half-believed us, but I guess he didn't want to risk getting in trouble with his boss. He probably felt guilty

for not reading a letter that had never been sent.

'Go ahead,' he said in the end, 'or you'll miss your train. But that electronic ticket thing will never last, you mark my words.'

Beth and I walked through the barrier and along the platform.

'This is one old-fashioned train,' I said. 'It looks like something out of the dark ages.'

'OMG,' said Beth. 'Dad made me watch a whole documentary about the guy who picked out the black and gold colours for these trains.'

'Sounds boring,' I said.

'Actually it wasn't too bad. The guy, I can't remember his name, got the idea from looking at his cat's fur. His cat was called Miss Mouse, and she was a bit of a celebrity back in the day.'

'That's kind of cool. Did the documentary give you any idea how to actually open the doors of the train? I can't see a button anywhere.'

Beth laughed as she reached up, turned a handle

and pulled the door towards her.

'So long, Humphrey,' she said as we climbed up the steps. 'Kilkenny, here we come!'

Chapter Fourteen

It was late by the time we got off the train in Kilkenny. We'd finished the biscuits ages ago, and I was really hungry. I wondered if there was any chance I'd be back home in time for a nice cup of hot chocolate and a toasted sandwich.

'Let's not waste any time,' said Beth, looking at the address her granny had given her. 'I'm going to ask someone how to get to this place.'

We went up to a woman who was running a newspaper stand.

'Oh,' she said when Beth showed her the piece of paper. 'Rosslee? I'm afraid that's a long way from here – probably ten miles or more.'

'And are there buses?' I asked.

The woman shook her head. 'No. It's only a tiny little place in the middle of nowhere.'

We thanked her and went to sit down on a bench. I felt like crying. We'd tried so hard and come so far, and still we weren't anywhere near where we needed to be.

'So what do you want to do now?' I asked.

'Go to see my mum, of course.'

'Was there something in those chocolate biscuits that suddenly made you love walking? Didn't you hear that woman back there? Your mum is ten miles away – and miles are longer than kilometres, remember?'

'So it's maybe fifteen or sixteen kilometres. That's nothing.'

'It's plenty when you haven't got a car or a bike or even a hoverboard.'

I was trying to be funny, but Beth didn't laugh.

For a minute I was mad at her.

Did she have any idea how tired and scared I was?

Couldn't she understand how badly I wanted to be at home?

How badly I needed one of my mum's hugs?

And then I remembered all the times lately when Mum and I had laughed at stupid stuff, and I'd noticed Beth sitting on her own, staring at us, like she didn't even know who we were.

And I thought about the time when Mum bought t-shirts for Beth and me, and mine was perfect because Mum knows exactly what I like, and even though Beth wore hers a few times, I knew she hated it, because Mum had no idea how allergic she is to the colour orange.

But before I could say anything else, Beth started to cry.

'We can't go back without seeing my mum,' she sobbed. 'We just *can't*.'

'I *want* to help you, Beth, honestly I do – but it's nearly eight o'clock. It's going to be dark soon. Even if we figure out a way to get to Rosslee, by the time we get there, your mum will probably be tucked up in bed for the night.'

'I know all that,' wailed Beth. 'I just ...'

And then she sobbed so hard I couldn't understand another word.

'Hey,' I said as I put my arms around her. 'Don't worry. We'll think of something.'

She looked at me with her huge blue eyes, and I knew I couldn't let her down.

'It's too late to get a train back home now anyway,' I said. 'And there's no hope of getting to Rosslee either, so I guess we're stuck here for the night. Why don't we find somewhere to sleep, and in the morning ... well, in the morning we'll figure something out.'

It had to be the vaguest plan in the history of the world, but it seemed to work.

Beth wiped her eyes with her sleeve and tried to smile.

'Thanks, Molly,' she said. 'You're the best.'

* * *

It was Friday, so the shops were open late, and there

were lots of people around.

'Do you think we'll be able to sleep in a school again tonight?' asked Beth as we walked down the main street.

'Yeah, like there's going to be another school that just happens to be open when we're walking past.'

'So what are we going to do?'

I didn't know how to answer. I was starting to feel afraid again. This was so not fun any more. All I wanted was to be somewhere warm and safe. I wanted my mum, but if I didn't come up with a proper plan, Beth was never, ever going to see hers – and how could I let that happen?

We walked to the end of the street and halfway back again and that was when it came to me – the greatest idea I'd ever had in my whole life.

'I have a plan,' I said, 'and it's going to be soooo much fun.'

'Tell me more.'

'I know where we're going to sleep tonight.'

'Where?'

I turned around and pointed. 'In there.'

Beth sighed. 'Is lack of food making you lose your mind?'

I shook my head.

'So how come you think we're going to sleep in a shop?'

'We'll sneak inside and hide, and then when everyone's gone home, and the shop is locked up, we can do what we like until the morning. I read about a guy who did this in London last year and I thought it was the coolest thing ever.'

'So what happened?'

'Well ... the burglar alarm went off, and the police came and well ... let's just say it didn't end well. But it's different for us. It's 1984, and since we left that school this morning, I've noticed that no one has burglar alarms. We'll be fine, Beth, and we'll be safe. No one will ever know we were there.'

'But ...'

'There's no but. It's a perfect idea.'

'Since you're so clever, why don't we hide somewhere nice, like a sweetshop?'

'Yeah, good idea. You could hide behind a lollipop, and no one'll ever see me if I stand behind a packet of Rolos.'

'I suppose you're right. Now tell me exactly how we're going to get away with it.'

And so, making it up as I went along, I told her my plan.

***

We waited until it was almost time for the shop to close, and then I led the way inside.

It was a huge hardware shop, perfect for what we needed. Beth and I walked around, pretending to be interested in the displays of garden tools, kitchen equipment, and packets of seed.

I grabbed a sweeping brush and stood behind it gig-

gling. 'Think anyone will find me?'

Beth held up a cleaning cloth and held it over her face. 'Am I invisible?' she said.

Then we both became serious. This *so* wasn't a laughing matter.

'Look,' I said, pointing to a sign saying, *Large Furniture Display on First Floor*. 'That's where we need to be.'

We went upstairs, all casual, like we were normal customers. In a corner of the huge room there were two bored-looking men sitting behind two matching desks. Neither of them looked up as Beth and I tiptoed past them. We kept walking until we got to the furthest end of the shop, where there were loads of big, ugly, dark wardrobes.

'Perfect,' I said, trying to sound confident.

Beth looked at her watch. 'The shop doesn't close for ten minutes. Is it too soon to hide?' she asked.

I didn't much like the idea of sitting inside a wardrobe for more than a few minutes, but hanging around

might have made the men suspicious.

'Let's do it,' I said, suddenly feeling adventurous. 'This is getting exciting. Maybe one of the wardrobes leads to Narnia.'

'Or home?'

Being at home sounded good to me, but I pushed that thought away. None of this was about me.

'Let's not joke about magic wardrobes!' I said. 'There's a customer coming up the stairs. Let's hide quickly while the men are distracted.'

So we pulled open the door of a huge brown wardrobe, and jumped inside. It smelled of dust and wood and varnish. Beth was trying to fully close the door, but I stopped her.

'Don't,' I said. 'We could suffocate, and, call me fussy if you like, but I don't really like the idea of dying in a smelly wardrobe in a funny old shop in 1984.'

Beth rolled her eyes, but she left the door open a crack, and we made ourselves as comfortable as possible as we settled down to wait.

Luckily the customer didn't hang around for long, and soon I could see the two shop assistants standing up.

'Another day over,' said the older one. 'Time for you to tidy up, Jack, and then we can get out of this place.'

'Yes, Patrick,' said Jack. 'If you say so.'

Both men started to walk towards us. Beth and I held our breath. Patrick wandered around the furniture, pointing out stuff like crooked chairs and dusty tables, and Jack rushed to put things straight.

'That old man's a lazy pig,' I whispered to Beth. 'Why doesn't he do anything?'

'Stop talking,' hissed Beth. 'He'll do something if he finds us hiding in his precious shop – and I bet it wouldn't be pretty!'

Soon the men were so close that I could see the gross sprinkling of dandruff on Patrick's collar and the greasy fingerprints on his glasses.

'Tell me, Patrick,' said Jack, 'have you seen that new girl, Diana, in the kitchen department downstairs?

She's pretty, isn't she?'

'You should be paying attention to your work,' said Patrick. 'You're not being paid to stare at pretty young girls.'

Jack spoke again. 'I'm ... er ... I mean ... I'm ... I'm thinking of asking her out.'

Now the older man laughed out loud. 'Ask her out? I've never heard such a foolish thing. Look at you in that cheap, shabby old suit. You're hardly love's young dream, are you? You don't really think a pretty girl like Diana would bother with the likes of you?'

Through the crack in the door, I could see the younger man go very red. 'N-n-no,' he said. 'I suppose you're right. I don't know what I was thinking. Diana is too good for me. It was a stupid idea.'

The older man laughed again – a mean kind of laugh. He slapped Jack on the back, so hard it must have hurt.

'It was a very stupid idea, Jack,' he said. 'I'd forget all about Diana if I were you.'

I felt like jumping out of the wardrobe and thumping him.

Why was he being such a bully?

Jack was shy and not very confident, but he was kind of cute. If he got his hair cut properly he might even be very cute. And his suit was shabby, but it looked good on him – in a cool, crumpled kind of way, like he was a rock star who wasn't trying very hard.

And now he was going to die of lost love for the beautiful Diana, and she would never even know.

How sad was that?

The men came closer, so I forgot all about Jack and Diana, and began to worry about Beth and me. Jack was walking directly towards us.

Did they check the wardrobes for hideaways every night?

Was this the end of everything?

All I wanted to do was help my friend to find her mum, and now ... I wished I was safe at home with Mum, but it was a bit late for that. I grabbed Beth's

arm and squeezed it tightly. She grabbed mine and squeezed even tighter. I put my other hand over my mouth to stop myself from crying out. I didn't dare to breathe. I felt sick, and my stomach was making horrid gurgling noises that I was sure could be heard in America.

Jack was centimetres away, standing right next to us. He'd definitely have seen us, except for the fact that the inside of the wardrobe was dark. Only trouble was, if he opened the door ...

Before I could finish thinking the awful thought, Jack reached out and caught the handle of the wardrobe. I held my breath as I waited for everything to go wrong.

'Can't you hurry up?' said Patrick, who was now sitting on a comfy-looking sofa. 'Why are you always so slow and lazy? I'd like to get home in time for my tea, if that's all right with you.'

I looked towards Beth. It was too dark to see her face properly, but I guess she didn't feel any better

than I did.

How were we going to talk our way out of this?

Maybe Jack was going to die of fright when he saw us.

Were Beth and I going to be arrested for murder, as well as hiding in a furniture shop?

Did children get sent to jail in 1984?

I was still holding my breath. I wondered if dying from stress was better or worse than dying from lack of oxygen.

And then Jack slammed the wardrobe door shut.

'No one's ever going to buy this wardrobe with the loose door,' he said.

'Well, why don't you fix it?' said Patrick. 'Do I have to do everything around here?'

Poor Jack didn't even reply to this. I could hear him walking away, and I was just starting to breathe again, when something terrible happened. Very slowly, both doors of the wardrobe began to swing open. Beth and I let go of each other's arms and each of us grabbed

for a door, but with nothing to grip, we both missed. With small squeaking noises the doors swung fully open.

Beth and I sat there, afraid to move, like rabbits in the headlights of a fast-approaching car. Luckily the two men had their backs to us and were walking towards the stairs. I tried not to think what would happen if one of them were to turn around. I held my breath again and watched as they went very slowly down the stairs. When they were gone, I turned to Beth and we hugged each other tightly.

'That was so scary,' I said. 'I actually thought I was going to die.'

Beth didn't answer, but her shaking arms gave me a good idea of how she felt.

* * *

Beth and I stayed in the wardrobe for ages, not even daring to lean out to close the doors. From downstairs

we could hear the sound of people getting ready to finish up work for the day. I couldn't help feeling jealous at the thought of having a home to go to, and maybe a nice meal, and a few hours of watching TV. Next to me, Beth was pale and serious-looking. I had no idea what she was thinking, but I guessed it was something to do with her mother. I smiled at her, but she didn't smile back.

Then there was the rattle of keys and the loud slam of a door, and all was quiet.

'We're locked in,' said Beth. 'And I'm guessing it's going to be a long night.'

We climbed out of the wardrobe and looked around. I'd often dreamed of getting locked inside a shop, but now that it had actually happened, I wasn't sure I liked it all that much. Everything seemed too quiet, and a bit scary.

'Let's explore,' I said, trying to sound upbeat.

I walked to the corner of the shop where there was a display of beds. I don't usually get all that excited about beds, but now it felt like years since I'd seen or slept in one.

'Bags I this one,' I said, as I dived on top of a big double bed and wrapped the huge quilt around me.

'Stop, Molly,' said Beth. 'You'll mess up the covers.'

'I totally don't care. We can fix it up again in the morning. Now which bed are you going to use?'

Beth sat on the edge of the bed next to mine. 'This

one's too hard,' she said.

'You sound like Goldilocks.'

Then Beth jumped onto my bed. 'This one seems just right,' she said. 'I'll sleep here with you, and protect you from any passing bears.'

We lay there for a while, without talking. After everything that had happened, it was kind of nice – lying cuddled up on a soft, cosy bed with my best friend.

After a while I sat up. 'It's too early to go to sleep,' I said. 'And besides, I'm starving. Let's go find some food.'

We soon discovered that finding food in a furniture shop isn't easy. We found a small kitchen corner, but there was only an empty teabag box in the cupboard.

Downstairs in the gardening section, I picked up some carrot seeds and read from the back of the packet. 'Ready to eat in just twelve weeks.'

'Great. Let's plant them now, and if we're not dead from starvation in twelve weeks, we can have a carrot

feast. Maybe a chicken will wander in and lay a few eggs, and we can make carrot cake.'

I sat on the stairs and put my head in my hands.

'I've never been this hungry in my whole entire life,' I wailed.

Beth sat beside me and put her arm around my shoulders. 'I knew we should have hidden in a sweet shop – or a supermarket. Imagine all that lovely food, just waiting to be eaten.'

I was trying not to imagine food – it just made me feel even more hungry. Worst thing was, we were trapped. All the doors and windows had been locked with keys, and I didn't like the idea of breaking a window to get out. Even if we could think of some- where to go, we couldn't get there till the morning.

Beth pulled my arm. 'Come on,' she said. 'We were rushing around before and maybe we missed some- thing. Let's search again. There must be food some- where. There has to be.'

After twenty minutes searching, we got lucky. Beth

was looking behind a display of fancy spoons when she called me.

'Quick, Molly, come here. Look what I've found.'

I raced over, hoping she'd found a bowl of yummy, hot, greasy chips. I guess it showed how hungry I was when my mouth started to water at the sight of a few shiny green apples.

Only problem was, the apples were in a big bowl.

And the bowl was on a coffee table.

And the coffee table was right in the middle of the window display.

There was no way we could reach the apples without climbing right into the shop window.

I peeped out. The street was still busy with groups of people strolling around – and everyone who passed slowed down to look in at the brightly lit window display.

'What's so special about this window?' I asked.

'I guess there isn't a whole lot to do around here,' said Beth. 'They haven't got mobile phones or com-

puters, remember. Window-shopping is probably the highlight of these people's lives.'

'But what about us? Are we supposed to starve to death while they walk up and down the street admiring tables and chairs and mops and buckets?'

'We'll just have to wait. Eventually people will go home to bed.'

'Lucky them!'

'And then the street will be quieter, and we can sneak into the display and take the apples without being seen.'

I wanted to argue, but I was too weak. We went back upstairs and I sat on our bed, trying not to sulk or cry or die of hunger. Beth had more energy than me. She searched around some cupboards and found a deck of cards.

'Snap,' she said. 'I'll deal.'

We played about a million games of Snap. I didn't enjoy the first one, and it got worse from there. It's hard to get excited about a card game when you keep

getting distracted by thoughts of chocolate cake and crisps.

After a while it began to get dark. Weird security lights came on in the shop, making everything look a sick greenish colour. I looked out the window to see what was happening.

'Looks like everyone's gone home,' I said. 'Come on, Beth, it's time to eat.'

I set off down the stairs and Beth followed me. 'How are we going to work this?' I asked. 'Have we got a plan?'

'You go into the window display and take the apples.'

'Why me?'

'Because you're smaller, so there's less chance of you being seen.'

'Last time I checked, I was just one-and-a-half centimetres smaller than you.'

'Oh well, in an emergency, every little bit counts.'

'That's a pathetic argument,' I said. 'But right now I don't really care. Wish me luck, and if I

don't make it back, tell my parents I love them.'
Beth rolled her eyes, and I set off on my mission.
I stepped closer to the window and peeped around
a plastic dummy. I took a deep breath and stepped
up onto the edge of the display. I looked carefully up
and down the street, but all appeared quiet. I edged
towards the apples and just as I was reaching down to
grab the bowl, a man and a woman came zig-zagging
down the street. The man was singing so loudly that
I could hear him through the thick glass of the shop
window. Then he saw me and he stopped singing. He
stood there for a second, wobbling like he'd just got
off a merry-go-round. He rubbed his eyes a few times
and then he looked at me again, with a confused look
on his face. I knew I had to act quickly, so when he
turned away to say something to the woman, I threw
myself onto a sofa and tried my best to look like a
shop-window dummy.

Now the man and the woman both looked in
through the window. The man looked like he'd seen

a ghost. (I wondered if I counted as a reverse ghost, since I wasn't supposed to be born yet.) The man was pointing at the place where I'd been standing before and saying something. The woman was shaking her head crossly. I didn't dare to move a muscle. I desperately wanted to blink, but managed somehow to resist. My nose itched like crazy, and I wished I could scratch it. Long, slow seconds passed.

In the end, the woman grabbed the man's arm and dragged him along the street. A few times, he turned to look back, and I didn't dare to move. When they were finally gone, I jumped up, scratched my nose and picked up the bowl of apples and escaped.

'OMG!' said Beth. 'That was totally, totally scary. I thought they were definitely going to—'

'But they didn't,' I said calmly, like it was no big deal. 'So everything's fine. Now, would you like an apple?'

It took me about ten seconds to eat the first apple.

Never before had an apple tasted so good.

And never before had I worked so hard to get one.

Chapter Sixteen

'Come on,' said Beth when we were both full of apples. 'If we don't do something I'm going to go crazy.'

'What are you thinking?'

'I don't know. Let's check the place out.'

So we wandered around the shop, looking at stuff.

That was totally fun – for about five minutes.

Then we went back upstairs and sat on our bed.

'Want to play Snap?' I asked.

She shook her head. 'If I never play Snap again, it'll be too soon. I'm so bored, I'm actually tempted to read my schoolbooks.'

I giggled. 'I've never been that bored,' I said, but after another ten minutes, I was beginning to think that Beth was right. Maybe reading a history book would be more fun than sitting there doing nothing.

Then I had an idea. 'My phone died a few hours ago,' I said. 'And weirdly no one seems to have left a charger lying around, but we could play a game on your phone for a bit.'

Beth shook her head. 'No. No games. Phone chargers aren't going to be invented for years and years and we have to save my battery in case ...'

'In case what?'

'Well, just in case.'

That wasn't much of an answer, but I could see by Beth's face that she wasn't going to change her mind. Right then, she was my only friend in the world, and I didn't want to fight with her.

'I keep thinking of that poor man, Jack,' she said. 'He seemed nice, and it sounds like he really likes that girl Diana. I wonder if he'll ever be brave enough to ask her out?'

'I doubt it. He seems really shy, and that other man, Patrick, has bullied him so much, I don't think he'll ever have the nerve. He's starting to believe that Diana

would never go out with him.'

'That's so sad. A beautiful romance – over before it's even had a chance to begin. What a waste of young love.'

I giggled. 'You read too many soppy novels,' I said.

Beth giggled too. 'Maybe I do. But unfortunately this isn't a novel, this is real life, and it doesn't look like poor Jack is going to live happily ever after. I bet if we come back here in thirty years' time, he'll still be trying to work up the courage to ask Diana out. I bet he ...'

'Stop,' I said suddenly. 'I've just had the best idea in the history of the world.'

* * *

A few minutes later we were sitting at Jack's desk, with a page torn from a notebook we'd 'borrowed' from an office downstairs. Soon we had written the perfect letter.

Dear Jack,

I've been watching you since I started to work here, and you seem really nice (much nicer than that cross old Patrick). I'm a bit shy, and I'm not brave enough to talk to you, but I'd like you to know that if you asked me to go out for coffee with you, I'd be very happy to say yes.

Yours sincerely

Diana (from the kitchen department.)

PS I really like that suit you wear.

PPS Please don't mention this note — even to me. As I said, I'm very shy, and I'm a bit embarrassed to be writing to you like this.

When we were finished, we folded the letter and put it onto Jack's chair, where he had to find it.

'D'you think it'll work?' asked Beth.

'I don't know. Maybe Jack will still be too shy to go downstairs and actually ask her.'

We thought for ages, and then we tore another page from the notebook.

Dear Diana,

I think you're really nice, and I love coming to work now that you are here. I want to ask you out, but I'm not brave enough. If you come upstairs and say 'Do you want to ask me something?' I will have to find the courage to do it.

With very best wishes

Jack (from the furniture department)

PS Please don't ever mention this note — even to me — it's too embarrassing.

We went back downstairs and found a book that said 'Diana's Order Book'.

'That's all we can do,' I said as I opened the book. 'Now it's up to them.'

'OMG,' said Beth. 'I've just thought of something awful.'

'What?'

'Maybe we shouldn't be messing with history.'

'How do you mean?'

'Well, we're not meant to be here, are we? We've just

sort of appeared.'

'And?'

'Well, maybe Jack and Diana were never meant to get together.'

'But he's so nice and he's lonely and ...'

'That's not the point. What if we change the past and get them together, and they get married and have a kid who grows up to invent some awful bomb that blows up the whole world? If that happens, it'll be all our fault.'

'But maybe they'll have a kid who invents the cure for cancer, or who stops all wars or ...?'

'Is it just me, or is all this stuff seriously freaky?'

'It's not just you. This is all much too hard to figure out. I wish we could Google it to see what we should do.'

'Well we can't Google it. We're on our own, so we'll just have to do what we think is best.'

'And making Jack happy is a good thing, right?'

'Right.'

So I slipped the note inside Diana's order book, closed it and put it back where we had found it.

'Done,' I said. 'For better or worse.'

* * *

'What are you thinking?'

It was half an hour later, and Beth was sitting on a big leather chair, staring at a shiny black old-fashioned phone.

'I'm starting to feel a bit scared. Maybe going to see my mum is the craziest thing I've ever thought of. Maybe I should just figure out a way of finding her number and calling her.'

'And what would you say?'

'Probably nothing – but at least I'd get to hear her voice. I think I'd like that. And then in the morning we could forget about trailing halfway across the country. We could just turn around and try to get home again.'

Going home really, really sounded like a plan. I was

fed up of 1984. I was fed up of being scared and lonely and hungry – but that wasn't the point.

'You're right, Beth,' I said. 'Trying to find your mum probably is the craziest thing you've ever thought of.'

Beth gave a sad smile and reached for the telephone. I put my hand on hers, stopping her.

'But if you don't find your mum,' I continued, 'you're going to regret it for the rest of your life, and I'm *sooo* not letting that happen. We've come a long way and we're so not going to settle for a dumb phone call. Tomorrow you and I are going to find your mum, and we're going to ...'

'We're going to what?'

'Well, I guess we can figure the rest out later.'

Beth hugged me. 'Thanks, Molly,' she whispered. 'Have I told you before that you're the best?'

'A couple of times.'

'Well, I'm saying it again. Now we'd better go to bed – tomorrow's going to be a big day.'

'OK, but first there's one more thing I want to do.

Help me to gather up the apple cores.'

Beth did as I asked and then I went to Patrick's chair and picked up the jacket he had left hanging there. I examined it carefully and found a big hole in the lining. (OK, so I found a small hole and poked at it with my finger until it turned into a big hole.) Then Beth and I stuffed all the apple cores as far as we could into the corners of the jacket, and put it back where we had found it.

'Ha,' I laughed. 'That'll teach him to mock poor Jack. He won't be so smart when these apples go all stinky and rotten, and flies start following him around the shop.'

Beth laughed too. It was nice to see her so happy, and that made me feel more adventurous.

'Hey,' I said. 'Let's go down and find a can of something really gross and gooey to rub all over Patrick's chair. When he sits on it, he'll ruin his clothes, and everyone will think he's pooped himself.'

But this time Beth didn't laugh.

'It's possible to go too far sometimes, you know,' she said in a really prissy voice.

I'd have been mad, except I knew she was right. Sometimes she's a much nicer person than I am.

* * *

Soon the two of us were snuggled up together under the huge quilt. It was cosy there, and it reminded me of when I was very little, and I used to climb into bed with Mum and Dad and Hippity. I gave a small sob. I wanted to go back home. I wanted to go back to a time when Mum and Dad loved each other, and everything was safe and warm and nice.

At home that morning, I'd thought I was all grown up, but now I felt like a little kid, lost and scared.

'Do you ever wish your life was different?' I asked.

'Every day,' said Beth. 'Every single day.'

Then she put her arms around me and hugged me until I fell asleep.

Chapter Seventeen

'Wake up, Molly!'

'Hey. Get off. Can't you see I'm trying to sleep here?'

'Shhhh,' she whispered. 'Don't you remember where we are? There are people downstairs, and I'm guessing they won't be happy if they find out that we spent the night here.'

'OMG, we're totally dead if they find us.'

I jumped out of bed like it was full of crazy zombies or something. We quickly straightened up the covers and piled up the fancy cushions that we'd flung on the floor the night before. The bed looked like it had been made by a messy two-year-old, but we didn't have time to worry about that as we rushed to pull on our shoes and our jackets.

While I shoved the last few apples into my school-bag, Beth grabbed her phone and then raced into the

toilets and filled up our water bottle.

'All ready?' she asked.

'I guess. I'd love another hour in that cosy bed, and then a big breakfast of pancakes with maple syrup and blueberries.'

'I'd settle for another twenty minutes in bed, and a slice of cold toast.'

'Ten minutes and a bowl of soggy corn flakes?'

Beth laughed. 'Dream on,' she said.

'Should we just walk downstairs casually, like we're customers?' I asked as I put my foot on the first step.

Beth pulled me back. 'Wait. The shop might not even be open yet. Maybe that's just the workers' voices that we heard.'

I leaned over the bannisters and realised that she was right. The big front door was still closed. We tip-toed into a corner behind a kitchen dresser and waited until we heard the rattling of keys. Shortly afterwards we heard the sound of the first customers coming into the shop and seconds later, Jack came upstairs. Beth

and I ducked behind a display of fluffy orange and purple cushions.

'I wonder where Patrick is?' she whispered.

'I hope he's got a few days off.'

'Why?'

'So when he gets back, the apple cores will be totally mouldy and stinky. Serves him right for being such a meanie.'

Jack went over to his desk, pulled out his chair and picked up the note Beth and I had left there. He unfolded it and began to read, and as he did so, I could see his face beginning to turn red. He gave a small smile, and then a big long sigh. He folded the letter again, put it into his pocket, and sat down at his desk.

'I knew it,' Beth whispered. 'I knew the poor boy wouldn't be brave enough to ask her out.'

'Lucky we thought of plan B then,' I whispered back. 'It's all up to Diana, now. Their happy-ever-after is in her hands.'

'I know, but we can't wait around to see what hap-

pens. We've got to get out of here before someone sees that messy bed and starts to wonder what happened here during the night.'

I was disappointed, but as usual, Beth was right.

As we headed for the stairs, Jack looked up with a puzzled expression on his face.

'Hello, girls,' he said. 'I didn't see you two come in. Did you spend the night here?'

OMG! How did he know?

Were we now in the biggest trouble ever?

Should we try to explain?

Or should we just make a run for it?

Then Jack smiled and I realised that he was joking.

'Ha, ha,' I said. 'Very funny. Isn't that funny, Beth? He thinks we spent the night here.'

Beth made a totally pathetic attempt at a laugh. 'Er ... ha, ha. What a crazy idea. I guess you didn't see us coming upstairs, because you were busy reading a letter or something.'

When she mentioned the letter, the poor man's face

went all red again.

'Anyway,' said Beth, 'we have to go now. Our mum and dad will be waiting for us.'

Just then a really pretty girl came up the stairs carrying the piece of paper we'd left in her order book. While we watched, she folded it up and slipped it into her pocket. She looked happy.

'Diana,' whispered Beth and I together.

'Diana,' said Jack, smiling so nicely that the big blush on his face didn't look too bad.

'Jack,' said Diana shyly. 'I know this sounds strange, but is there something you'd like to ask me?'

He went even redder, but he was still smiling.

'Actually there is,' he said. 'You know that new coffee shop on Prince's Street – I was wondering if ...?'

'I think we can leave them to it,' said Beth, as she grabbed my arm and dragged me down the stairs and out into the fresh air.

* * *

We were sitting on a bench in a small park, and I was trying to figure out a way to tell Beth that even though a whole night had gone by, I still had no idea how we were going to get to Rosslee.

'Have you figured out a way to get to Rosslee yet?' she asked, like she could read my mind.

'I'm sorry, Beth,' I said. 'I've been thinking and thinking but I can't ...'

'That's OK,' she said. 'Don't worry about it. I've got a great idea.'

'You have?'

'Well, do you remember what I said the other day?'

'You said lots of things the other day.'

'Well, I mean the thing about walking to find my mum.'

I nodded. 'Yeah, I remember that – but you were joking.'

'That's true. I was joking then, but I'm not now. We've already done most of the journey.'

'Technically, yes, but we've still got ten miles to go.'

'That's nothing.'

I walked ten kilometres once for charity, and it nearly killed me. The blisters on my feet didn't heal for ages. One of them got infected, and gross green stuff poured out of it for three days.

'It would take us hours and hours to walk it,' I said.

'I know. So we should probably get started.'

'But even if we decided to do that crazy, impossible thing you're suggesting, how would we find the way? Remember that woman said Rosslee is in the middle of nowhere, so there probably won't be anyone we can ask for directions – and I'm guessing Google maps hasn't been invented since yesterday.'

'So you're saying that until Google maps came along, everyone just stumbled around with no idea where they were going?'

'I don't know, do I? I'm a twenty-first century girl.'

She rolled her eyes. 'Ever hear of signposts? Come on, Molly, let's not waste any more time. Let's get going.'

I looked carefully at her.

What had happened to my best friend?

'What's going on here?' I asked. 'You're supposed to be the sensible one in this relationship, so why are you coming up with this crazy idea?'

She sighed. 'I'm not sure really. All I know is, I want to see my mum. I want that more than anything I've ever wanted in my whole life, and if we go back home, then it's not going to happen. Ever. This is it. This is the only chance I'm ever going to get.'

'I understand, Beth,' I said, even though I didn't really understand at all. 'But walking all the way to Rosslee? That's just freaky.'

Beth stood up. 'We can do it,' she said. 'And in a weird way, I feel that we should. Everything happens for a reason, you know.'

'It does?'

'Yes. I don't think it was an accident that we wandered into Rico's shop. Remember how weird he was?'

'I'll never forget how weird he was.'

'It's like he was part of a plan.'

'What kind of a plan?' I asked, not sure that I liked where this conversation was going. Stuff like this always freaks me out.

'I think Rico sent us back to 1984 just so I could see my mum.'

'You know I'm not into all that fate and destiny stuff.'

'You don't have to believe,' she said. 'I can do all the believing, and you just have to come along with me.'

'I guess. But in your master plan ... after we've met your ... well, after ... you know ... afterwards ... what do you think's going to happen then?'

'We'll find our way back to the shopping centre, and we'll find the door into Rico's weird shop and then we can get back home. You do want to get home, don't you?'

'Of course I do. But are you forgetting that we couldn't find the door the other day? We looked for ages and ages, but it was like it had vanished into thin

air. What makes you think that it's going to magically reappear?'

'I know this is going to sound totally weird, but ...'

'But what?'

'But I feel like this is all some kind of quest.'

'No offence, Beth, but you're right, that is kind of weird.'

She looked hurt.

'But don't let that stop you,' I said. 'Sometimes weird is good.'

'It's kind of hard to explain, but it's like I have to do something to prove that I deserve this opportunity. If I show that I'm strong enough to make this journey, then I'll get to see my mum, and that's the thing I want most in the whole world. It's the thing I've always wanted. And when I've done that, the two of us can find the door and go back home again.'

I wasn't sure that what she was saying made a whole lot of sense, but how could I argue when it meant so much to her?

'So what exactly are you suggesting?'

'We'll start walking now, and we'll keep on going until we get to Rosslee.'

It still couldn't be as simple as she made it sound.

'You don't even like walking. Last time your dad asked you to walk to the shop you threw a complete hissy fit.'

'That was different. It's hard to get excited about walking down the road to buy a packet of fish fingers. This is totally different. We should see it as an adventure.'

'You don't like adventures,' I said.

'I do now,' she said, and then she laughed. Despite all the tears she'd shed over the past few days, Beth looked happier than I had ever seen her before. 'Please,' she said. 'Please do this very special thing with me, Molly.'

And how could I say no to that?

So I picked up my schoolbag.

It looked like my best friend and I were going for a walk.

Chapter Eighteen

It was a lovely sunny day. At first it was kind of nice, just Beth and me, walking along in the sunshine. It would have been totally fantastic, except that my schoolbag felt like it was full of bricks, and I thought my back was going to break in two.

I was still carrying the water and the biscuits, and, even though they were slowing me down a bit, there was no way I was letting them go.

'Pretend you're in the army,' said Beth when I complained.

'If I ever join the army, you've got to promise to shoot me.'

'Sure – scout's honour.'

I smiled to myself.

What was one more empty promise?

***

And so our walk continued.

'What's with the orange cars?' I said, when the third one passed us.

'No idea. The cars around here are so weird. They're all square and clunky, and the colours are like something a little kid would choose. I saw a purple one earlier. Who'd ever want a purple car?'

'Not my mum anyway. Her cars are always silver – totally boring, but at least it's safe to look at them without wearing sunglasses.'

We kept walking and I was relieved that nobody was paying us any attention. I guess the people passing by thought we were just two ordinary girls walking home from school.

How could they have guessed that we were two girls, lost in time, setting out on the longest walk of our lives?

Every few minutes, Beth pulled out her phone,

looked at it, and put it back into her pocket.

'Face it, Beth,' I said. 'It's not going to work. Mobile phones aren't going to be invented any time soon – and even if they were, who would you call? None of our friends are born yet.'

She sighed. 'I know. You're right. But not having my phone working makes me nervous.'

'Me too,' I admitted. 'How on earth did people live before mobile phones? If they got separated from their friends at a concert or something, how would they ever find them again?'

'And if they were on holidays and they saw a totally hot guy, how would they take a sneaky picture and send it to their friends back home?'

'How did they even live?'

'I can't bear to think about it.'

After what felt like a hundred miles, Beth allowed us to stop. We sat down and drank from our bottle of water, and ate an apple each. I wanted to ask Beth what she planned to eat for the rest of our journey,

but something told me I wouldn't be happy with her answer. I had a horrible feeling that, even if Beth was half-dead from tiredness and hunger, she'd still try to crawl the rest of the journey towards her lost mother.

After a bit, we picked ourselves up and started to walk again. Soon we came to a small village.

'Hey,' said Beth, running towards the small phone box on the side of the road, 'I've just remembered something.'

'I've remembered something too,' I said as I ran after her. 'We haven't got any 1984 money, and we still haven't got anyone to call.'

She pulled the door of the phone box open. 'I'm not making a call,' she said. 'But my dad once told me that back in the day, he and his friends used to check inside phone boxes whenever they passed one. People were always leaving coins there. He's forever going on about the time he found two pounds, and spent it all on sweets.'

She rattled the slot and turned away disappointed.

'Nothing,' she said. 'A big fat nothing. If I ever see my dad again, remind me to never, ever believe any of his stupid stories about his stupid childhood.'

We picked up the phone books and shook them, but the only thing that fell out was a gross dirty tissue and a flyer for an agricultural fair.

'Sorry,' she said.

'Oh, don't worry about it. For a minute there I thought we mightn't starve to death after all, but it looks like I was wrong. It's no biggie.'

'Sorry,' she said again.

This time I didn't answer. I needed to save my energy for walking.

* * *

Lots of people were out walking, and after a while I stopped noticing the funny hair and the weird clothes. They were all just people like Beth and me, busy getting on with their lives.

Once we saw a woman in a garden hanging out her washing, while two laughing children cycled in circles around her.

Another time we could see into a kitchen where a woman was taking a big cake from the oven and putting it on a wire rack in the middle of the table. I wanted that to be my mum. I wanted to run inside and hug her and never let her go. I wanted to touch the warm cake, and have her pretend to be cross, and warn me about washing my hands. I wanted to sit at the table, and wait for Mum to bring me a glass of milk and a huge slice of warm, sweet cake. I wanted to tell her about my day, and ...

But it wasn't my mum, and even if it was, how could I possibly tell her about my day?

I was with my best friend in the world, but still I felt lost and alone.

* * *

We didn't stop walking for ages and ages. I was starving, and my feet were starting to hurt. When at last we reached another tiny village, I saw a dog standing in a doorway, chewing on a big meaty bone. Every now and then he stopped chewing and licked his lips. He looked as happy as a dog can look.

I stopped walking and folded my arms.

'Beth,' I said, 'we've got to do something. I'm so hungry, I'm jealous of that dog.'

'There's a phone box just up there,' she said. 'Maybe this is going to be the lucky one.'

I rolled my eyes and didn't bother following her. I sat on the kerb and watched the dog, wondering how hungry I'd have to be before I'd wrestle him for a nibble of his scabby bone.

A second later, Beth was back with a funny seven-sided coin in her hand.

'OMG!' she said. 'Dad was right – it actually worked. Look what I found on the floor of the phone box. We're rich – I think.'

I took the coin from her and turned it over in my hand.

'It says 50p,' she said. 'I wonder if that's a lot of money?'

'One way to find out. There's a shop just up there. I wonder how much crisps cost in 1984? Maybe we'll be able to buy ten packets – or even more. Oh, Beth, I can taste them already.'

Beth quickly took the coin back from me and put it into her pocket.

'If we spend this money, we'll have nothing,' she said.

'If we don't spend it, you won't even have a best friend. I'll be dead from lack of food.'

'Why do you always have to be such a baby?'

Suddenly I couldn't help myself. I flung out my hand and whacked her hard on the face. For a minute, neither of us said anything. I watched as the print of my fingers appeared on her cheek. I had never, ever done anything like that before. Beth and I were stuck

in the middle of 1984, but I wished I could roll time back to a few minutes earlier, so I'd have the chance not to hit my best friend.

Beth's face was all red and sore-looking, but I was the one who started to cry. She leaned over and hugged me. When I realised that she wasn't mad at me, I felt even worse.

When she apologised, I wanted to curl up into a little ball and die.

'I'm sorry, Molly,' she said. 'All this is my fault. This whole stupid thing was my idea – and it was a crazy idea. We can turn back if you want.'

'And do what?'

'We can go back to that shopping centre and try to find our way home.'

'But what about your mum? If we turn back, you're never going to see her.'

Now tears came to her eyes too, and I knew what I had to do.

'Let's keep going,' I said as I wiped away my te

'I'm so sorry for hitting you, and I'm sorry for being such a baby.'

'That's OK,' she said. 'Now let's go buy some food.'

* * *

A bell jangled over our heads as we went into the shop. It was weird – everything in the shop was old-fashioned, like it came from a museum or something, but still it was all shiny and new.

There was a stack of comics on the wooden counter.

'OMG!' I said when I picked one up. 'It's *Bunty*. Mum's forever going on about how she read this every week. I guess she had an empty life, if this was the highlight of it.'

'Maybe you should buy a copy to bring back to her?'

For a minute I felt sad. Beth was always so thoughtful, and yet she'd never once been able to buy a present for her mother.

'That's so nice of you, Beth,' I said. 'But it costs 27

pence – that's more than half our money. I'm hoping an alive daughter is more important to my mum than an ancient old comic with a weird story about a flower show on the cover.'

'I guess. Let's see how much food costs nowadays.'

We raced around the shop checking prices and soon discovered that you can't buy a whole lot of food with fifty pence. It wasn't even enough to buy a loaf of bread.

Then I saw a basket in a corner near the window. It was piled high with packets of biscuits. Best of all, there was a sign saying, Special offer – Biscuits – two packets for 40p.

Usually Beth and I can argue for hours about what kind of biscuit is the nicest, but this was no time for arguing. We each grabbed a packet and handed them to the old lady who was sitting behind the shop counter. She smiled at us, showing that loads of her teeth were missing. I wondered if she lost them from eating too many packets of cheap biscuits.

'Just to warn you,' she said in a lispy voice 'You'd

better eat those biscuits up quickly. They're out of date tomorrow. That's why they're so cheap.'

I couldn't help giggling. If the biscuits were out of date in ten minutes' time it wouldn't have mattered to me. I planned to eat every single one within the next five minutes.

Beth paid for the biscuits, and looked at the ten-pence coin the shopkeeper handed to her.

'What can we buy with this?' she asked.

'Twenty jelly sweets,' suggested the shopkeeper, pointing at a line of big jars.

'Thanks, but we want real food,' I said.

The old woman chuckled. 'Now there's a rare thing,' she said. 'Children who don't want sweets. Only trouble is, you can't buy much real food with 10p. What had you in mind?'

I looked around the shop.

What had I in mind?

Where should I start?

A big bowl of tomato soup?

A plate full of stew?

A bowl of corn flakes with lashings of ice-cold milk?

A ...

Suddenly I saw that on a shelf behind the counter there was a plate with a sandwich on it – a huge sandwich stuffed with what looked like chicken and salad.

'How much is it for that sandwich?' I asked.

The woman chuckled again. 'That's not for sale,' she said. 'That's my lunch.'

I bit my lip to try to hold back the tears. The sandwich looked so delicious, and I hadn't had anything proper to eat for ages and ages.

Then the woman turned towards me. 'You really want that sandwich, don't you?'

'Well, we are kind of hungry,' I said. 'You see ...'

I didn't know how to go on, but luckily Beth helped me out.

'We've been out walking,' she said. 'Kind of like an adventure trip. And my dad made us some sandwiches, but we lost them, and we're not going to get

back home for ages and ...'

The woman leaned over and patted her hand. 'You poor little things. I remember what it was like to be young and always hungry. You can have the sandwich.'

I was really, really happy to hear that, but still I felt kind of mean.

'But it's your lunch,' I said. 'We couldn't ...'

'My grandson is a very lazy boy,' said the woman. 'Not like you two lovely girls. He's probably sitting in the back room watching rubbish on television. I'll ask him to make me another sandwich – it'll give him something to do.'

She put the sandwich into a paper bag, and then counted out about fifty jelly sweets and threw them into another bag. She took the ten-pence coin from Beth and put it into the old-fashioned till, then she seemed to change her mind and took it out again.

'Let's call this my little treat to two such sweet girls,' she said as she handed us the bags and the money. 'Off you go and I hope you have a nice day.'

'Oh, we certainly will,' I said, as Beth and I skipped out of the shop. 'Thank you so, so much.'

We sat on a bench at the edge of the village and shared the sandwich – even the hard black crusts. It was the nicest thing I have ever, ever tasted. When it was finished, I licked my fingers, then I licked the bag and then I licked my fingers again. Then I ate half a packet of biscuits and a few jellies. Then I stood up.

'How far more do we have to go?'

'We passed a signpost just back there. I think it's about five kilometres.'

'That's nothing to us,' I said. 'We'll be there in no time.'

Chapter Nineteen

'*H*ave you decided what you're going to say?' I asked.

'To who?'

I knew she was only pretending not to understand, but I didn't give her a hard time. 'To your mum, of course.'

'Oh. Not really. I'm kind of hoping that I'll think of something when I get there.'

I had a horrible picture of Beth, her mum and me, all standing together struggling for something to say.

Were we going to end up talking about the weather, or politics or something?

Were we going to take turns telling each other about the weirdest dreams we've ever had?

'My mum always says that when you're stuck for something to say, you should ask questions about the

other person,' I said. 'She says everyone loves to talk about themselves.'

'That makes a lot of sense. Your mum always gives really good advice.'

Now I felt bad. 'Your mum would have been like that too,' I said. 'If only ...'

She smiled. 'Yeah, probably.'

Then I had a really, really scary thought. 'You mustn't tell your mother who we are,' I said.

'But—'

'No "buts" allowed. You have to promise me. This is actually happening to us, and still we can hardly believe it. Your mother will never, ever understand. She'll just think we're crazy, or weird or something. You don't want your own mother to think you're weird, do you?'

'But—'

'You have to promise me, Beth,' I said. 'If you don't promise, I'm turning around right now.'

I stood up and faced the way we had come, just so she could see I was serious.

'Promise me,' I said again. 'Or else I'm out of here.'

'I guess you're right. I won't say anything.'

'And don't tell her where we're from either. If she hears that we live so close to her home, she's going to get suspicious. She'll wonder how come she doesn't know us, or how come we don't know a single one of her friends.'

'What if she asks?'

'We'll say we're from Dublin, OK?'

'I guess. Anything else?'

'There's one more thing you need to think about before we go any further,' I said.

'What?'

I hesitated. This was the hard bit.

'Aren't you afraid that you might feel worse after you've met your mum?'

'No way. I'm absolutely certain I'm doing the right thing. I probably shouldn't complain, because Dad's been really great, but all my life, I've felt kind of cheated because I never knew my mum.'

'Yeah, but at the moment, you don't really know what you've been missing. Afterwards though—'

She didn't let me finish.

'Do you remember when that lady your mum knows who died last year?' she asked.

'Aideen?'

'Yes, that's her. And do you remember how everyone felt sorry for her son?'

'Yeah.'

'And I felt sorry for him too. It was really, really sad, but part of me kept thinking, I'd prefer to be him. At least he knew what his mum was like. He knew what she smelled like. He knew what her voice and her laugh were like. He knew what it was like to be hugged and tickled and cuddled by her. He knew all the things I'll never know.'

'But doesn't that make it harder for him? Isn't it worse, missing someone you know?'

'I don't think so. Look at it like this, Molly. Imagine you were invited to a party, and it was going to be

the best party ever. There was going to be jugglers and acrobats and nail bars and chocolate fountains and three totally cool boybands taking turns to sing. Can you imagine that?'

'Yeah, I can imagine it. It sounds amazing.'

What I couldn't imagine was where this story was going. I couldn't say that though, because Beth was looking all intense and scary.

'So if you asked your mum could you go to the party, and she gave you a choice, what would you do?'

'What's the choice?'

'Would you prefer her to say you couldn't go to the party at all, or that you could go for an hour?'

'Well, duh. I'd prefer to go for an hour of course.'

'Well, that's my point. You'd be really sad when the time came to leave the party, but at least you'd have seen the jugglers and heard the boybands and tasted the chocolate. You'd have something to remember for the rest of your life. And later, when all your friends talked about how cool the party was, you'd be able

to say "Oh, yeah, I remember that." That's all I want, Molly – a few memories. Is that so much to ask?'

'No,' I whispered. 'That's not too much at all.'

Chapter Twenty

Walking through the countryside was totally boring. After a while all the fields and the hedges started to look the same.

'OMG!' I said after a bit. 'Look at that cow with the black spots and the crooked tail. We've definitely seen her before – and the the one with the plain white ear.'

Beth giggled. 'You think they're following us?'

'Maybe. They look too innocent. I bet the same few are tip-toeing along behind us, and casually stopping to eat grass every time we look at them.'

'Nice thought, but I think you're being paranoid. And anyway, enough about cows, already. Save your energy for walking.'

And so our walk continued. Sometimes Beth was all jiggy and excited, and she practically galloped along the road. Other times, her feet dragged, and it was

almost like she didn't want to get to Rosslee after all.

I knew she was afraid.

* * *

After a bit we came near another small village.

'Wow,' said Beth. 'Shops. Houses. People. Be careful, Molly, in case the excitement is too much for us.'

The two of us walked a bit faster and soon we were in the centre of the action. We stopped outside a chemist shop and looked in the window. Everything looked old-fashioned, which was weird because it was all sparkly and new.

'No point looking into shop windows when you haven't got any money,' said Beth. She was starting to walk away when I grabbed her arm.

'OMG,' I said. 'Look. There in the corner.'

'If it's not a sign saying 'FREE FOOD HERE', I don't think I'm interested,' she said, still walking.

I pulled her back. 'I can't believe it. It's Smitty!'

'What?'

'Smitty. It used to be Mum's favourite perfume back in the day. She was going on about it the other day, or today or ... well, whenever I saw her last. If I got her some of that I think she'd love me forever.'

'She's your mum. She's going to love you forever no matter what you do.'

'Yeah, well you know what I mean. Let's go in.'

There was a woman sitting behind the counter, and when she saw us, she gave a big happy smile, like we were the first customers she'd seen all day.

'Well, hello, girls,' she said. 'And what can I do for you?'

'I saw the bottle of Smitty in the window,' I said.

'Is that still there?' asked the woman, like she had no idea what could possibly be in the window of her own shop. 'It's the last one, you know.'

'My mum loves it, and I was wondering how much it costs,' I said, suddenly feeling stupid. I only had 10 pence, and what were the chances that was enough for

a whole bottle of perfume?

'Oh, that's two pounds fifty,' the woman said.

Poor Mum. All she ever wanted was a quiet life. First her husband skipped off to darkest Africa, and now her only daughter had vanished into the past, and couldn't afford to buy her the one present she would have loved. I turned to walk out of the shop. 'Thanks anyway,' I said, 'but I'm sorry. I haven't got that much money.'

'Dear me,' said the woman. 'That is a pity – and you were trying to buy a nice present for your mammy. Why don't I have a look to see if I have a little sample I could give you to keep you going until you have saved enough money to buy the whole bottle?'

Beth and I admired the shelves which were full of brightly-coloured soaps on ropes and bottles of bubble bath in the shape of cartoon characters we'd never heard of. While we were doing this, the woman emptied a drawer onto the countertop. She rooted through the stuff, and after ages she clapped her hands.

'I knew it was there somewhere,' she said. 'Mind you it's been there a long time – I hope it hasn't gone off.

She handed me a tiny sample-sized bottle. It said 'Smitty' and there was a big red circle beside the name. I took off the lid and sniffed. It was nice, all sweet and flowery. Then I carefully put the lid back on and put the bottle safely in my pocket.

'That's really kind of you,' I said. 'Thanks so much.'

'You're most welcome,' she said. 'Your mother is a lucky woman to have a thoughtful daughter like you. And don't forget to come back and buy her the whole bottle when you've saved up enough money. I'll put it aside for you.'

'I won't forget,' I said, wondering if I'd be back in that village, or in 1984, ever again.

Chapter Twenty-One

'Look,' said Beth. 'There's a woman walking her dog. Let's ask her.'

I was so happy, I felt like running over and hugging this random dog-walker. Beth and I had been lost for ages and ages. We'd been wandering up and down country roads, with no idea which way we should be going. It felt like half a lifetime since we'd seen a car or a bus or anything with wheels (except a broken-down tractor, which probably didn't count).

Luckily, the dog-walking woman didn't ask any awkward questions when we told her what house we were looking for.

'Oh,' she said. 'That's not far at all, at all. You have to go up to the next junction, turn left, and then take the next right. The Phelans live a little way along the lane. It's the house with the red door. You can't miss it.'

A little way along the lane doesn't sound like very far, but when you've walked as far as we had, it felt like a thousand kilometres. It didn't help that Beth wasn't galloping along like a crazy girl any more. Now she was walking really, really slowly, like she was on her way to be executed or something.

'Please, Beth,' I said. 'Can't you walk a tiny bit faster? I know you're nervous, but ...'

I didn't finish my sentence, as we came around a small bend and saw a pretty old farmhouse a few hundred metres away.

'OMG,' whispered Beth as she stared at the house. 'I recognise this place.'

'You've been here before?'

'No, but we used to have a photograph of it in our old house. I always thought it was like something out of a history book. I never thought of it as an actual real place, with real people living in it.'

Her mouth was half-open and she looked kind of stunned, like someone had cast a spell over her.

'We did it, Molly,' she said. 'We really did it. We're here at last.'

Long minutes passed.

'Er, Beth ...' I said. 'What do you want to do now?'

'We'll go up to the house and see if my mum is there.'

She took a step forward and then turned back again, running her hands through her not-very-clean hair.

'Do I look OK?'

'Lovely. Except – no offence, Beth, but your face is kind of dirty.'

She rubbed her face with her sleeve.

'Better?'

'Worse, actually. Now you've just spread out the dirt.'

She gave a big sigh. 'Time for drastic measures. You'll have to do that thing your mum used to do when you were small.'

'That totally gross thing?'

She nodded. 'Yeah, that one. It's an emergency.'

So I took a tissue from my pocket, spat on it, and

then used it to wipe Beth's face. Even though she's a few months older than me, for a minute I felt like she was a little girl getting ready for a big adventure. She looked at me with her huge blue eyes, trusting me to make everything work out. I felt like I was in charge, and that making her happy was all up to me.

'Ready?' I asked.

She nodded.

'Come on so,' I said. 'Time to make things happen.'

Then, trying to act braver than I felt, I led the way towards the farmhouse.

* * *

A huge, friendly sheepdog came along the lane to meet us. We both stroked her, and then she turned and walked back towards the house, like she wanted us to follow her. For a second I thought Rico had sent the dog to help us, almost like she was leading us on the last part of our long journey – but I pushed the

thought away. This whole thing was weird enough without dragging in magical guide dogs sent by creepy guys with bright green and gold eyes.

The next few minutes were totally strange, as Beth and I followed the dog in silence. It was like the world had slowed down, and everything was happening in a brighter, clearer way. I felt like I was watching a movie, and I was part of it too.

Next to the farmhouse was a huge old tree.

The tree had one wide branch which swept lower than all the others, like it was trying to touch the ground it had come from.

There was a swing hanging from the low-growing branch.

On the swing there was a girl.

The girl was facing away from us, and as the swing went forwards, she threw back her head, letting her long, long black hair trail the ground beneath her. I thought about the tired, wild-haired woman in the photo Beth keeps next to her bed.

'Is that ...?' I whispered, hardly daring to finish the sentence.

'It's hard to tell from here. I've only seen photographs, remember,' whispered Beth back. 'Most of them are in my granny's house, and I haven't looked at them for ages. But she's about the right size, and her hair looks like I expected, and—'

Just then the girl flung her head back even further ... and she saw us.

She jumped off the swing and walked towards us. The swing continued its forwards and backwards arc, squeaking as it went.

With each squeak, the girl came closer, and I felt sicker.

One look at Beth told me all I needed to know.

Her pale face made it seem like she had just seen a ghost.

'You frightened me,' the girl said.

She didn't sound angry – just surprised.

'But it's OK. Flossie seems to like you, and she's a

good judge of character.'

Beth reached out and caught my hand for a second. Her hand was damp and shaky. I squeezed it hard, wondering if that could be any comfort to her at a moment like this.

At first glance, the girl looked nothing like Beth. Her hair and skin were completely the wrong colour. Beth is skinny and wiry, but this girl was solid and strong-looking. And then, as she stopped in front of us, I gasped.

I looked from one girl to another, moving my head from side to side like a spectator at a tennis match.

How could they not see?

How could they fail to notice that they were staring at each other with identical huge, pale-blue eyes?

'I'm sorry,' I said. 'We didn't mean to scare you.'

The girl smiled. 'That's OK. It's nice to see other human beings. It's just me and my granny and grand-dad here – much too quiet for me. Oh, I'm Fiona, by the way.'

'My name is Molly,' I said. 'And this is Beth.'

'Beth,' she said. 'That's my favourite name.'

Beth took Fiona's hand and held it for a long time. A very long time.

This had to be the saddest moment of my entire life. Beth was holding the hand of the mother she never knew, while Fiona was looking at the beloved little girl that she never got to see grow up.

Beth looked like she was going to cry.

I felt like I was going to cry.

Fiona looked at Beth, probably wondering if she was ever going to get her hand back.

I put my hands over my face, hardly daring to look.

This had to be a huge mistake.

Why had I let Beth persuade me that it was a good idea?

Suddenly Beth gave a weird choky noise that might have been a sob. She let go of Fiona's hand and took a step backwards.

'I can't do this,' she muttered. 'I've got to get out of

here.'

'I'll go with you,' I said.

Beth shook her head. 'No. I need to be on my own for a minute.'

Before I could argue, she raced off down the lane, and Fiona and I were left staring at each other.

'Is she going to be all right?' asked Fiona. 'And what's wrong with her anyway? Is she sick or something?'

How could I even begin to explain?

The truth was out of the question, but even though I'm not bad at lying, I was struggling a bit. How could I think of a believable lie – one that didn't make Beth seem like a total idiot? (I suddenly realised that I really, really wanted Fiona to like Beth.)

'She's not usually like this,' I said. 'Usually she's bright, and funny, and clever, and she's really brave, and she's really good at all kinds of stuff that I'm use-less at, and she's great at remembering jokes ... but ...'

'But what?' asked Fiona.

'But she's had a very hard time lately. She ...' I racked

my brains, and then the words rushed out, before I had time to decide whether they were suitable or not. 'She's been acting weird because her mum died.'

At least it wasn't a lie.

'Oh, the poor thing,' said Fiona. 'No wonder she's feeling so sad. It must be awful to grow up without a mum. Did she die recently?'

Not exactly.

In some ways she's not dead yet.

In some ways, she's very much alive.

She's standing right in front of me asking a whole heap of awkward questions.

'Well … yes … sort of.'

Now Fiona looked like she was going to cry too.

'That's very sad. Maybe we should go after her and see if she's all right?'

I shook my head. 'No offence, but I think it's best if I go on my own.'

'Of course. That was stupid of me – she wouldn't want a stranger around at a time like this.'

How could I say the words that sprang into my head?

You're not a stranger to her.

You're her ...

Fiona was smiling. 'When Beth is feeling better, if you both want to come back ...'

I smiled back at her. 'Let's just see how things turn out.'

Then I turned around and went to look for my friend.

Chapter Twenty-Two

I found Beth halfway down the lane. She was sitting on a low stone wall, playing with her hair and gazing into space. She looked pale and sad.

I sat down and put my arm around her.

'I should have listened to you, Molly,' said Beth. 'This is a total disaster. She must think I'm an idiot. She's probably gone in to tell her grandparents about the creepy, loser girl who's hanging around outside. Maybe she's gone to call the police.'

I shook my head. 'She won't do that. I told her that you're really nice.'

'And how did you explain the fact that I ran off, sobbing like a crazy person?'

'I ... I told her that you were upset because your mum died. I hope you don't mind. She was staring at me and I couldn't think of anything else to say. And

it is sort of the truth. And I just ... well, I wanted her to like you.'

'Thanks, Moll.'

'I'm so sorry, Beth. All of this is my fault. I know you wanted it so badly, but I shouldn't have let you do it. I should have known better. I should have known that it was too hard.'

Beth nodded slowly. 'You're right. It *is* too hard. It's harder than I could ever have imagined.'

I tried not to sound too relieved. 'So we can ...'

'I don't care how hard it is, though – I'm going to do it anyway.'

'But ...'

Beth turned and looked at me. 'You're my best friend, Molly, and you know me better than anyone else does, but even you can't understand how I feel – not really. I have to go back. I have to see Fiona again. I have to talk to her.'

'But ...'

'I *have* to take advantage of this once-in-a-lifetime opportunity.'

'But ...' It was the only word I was able to say.

Beth laughed a small, forced laugh. 'How could I give up now? I haven't even had a chance to ask her what her favourite colour is.'

She jumped off the wall. 'Coming?'

'You're the bravest person I've ever known,' I whispered.

'I couldn't do it without you,' she whispered back, and then the two of us walked slowly back down the lane.

* * *

Fiona was on the swing again, but now she was facing the laneway, and as soon as she saw us, she jumped down and came towards us. She brushed her hair off her face and smiled like she was really glad to see us.

She smiled like she didn't care that her new friends were wearing clothes that weren't going to be fashionable for thirty years.

She smiled like she didn't care that neither of us had showered for days.

Beth took a deep breath. 'I'm sorry for running off like that. I was a bit upset, but I don't want to talk about it, if you don't mind.'

Fiona looked at me and smiled. 'Of course I don't mind. Now do you want to come into the garden and sit down for a while?'

* * *

'I come here to stay with my grandparents every summer,' said Fiona as soon as we were settled on a rug that was spread out in the shade of the tree. 'It's funny I've never seen you two before. Do you live in the village?'

'Er ... no, we don't live around here,' I said. 'We live in Dublin ...'

Suddenly, the great story I had planned during the night seemed a bit stupid – but everyone was looking

at me, and I couldn't come up with a better one.

So I continued. 'You see, Beth and I are in the girl guides, and we're doing this ... adventure thing ... to earn a special survival badge. And we have to walk somewhere, without any help from anyone. So we had to walk from Dublin to here.'

'You walked all the way from Dublin? That's crackers.'

'Not really,' said Beth. 'When you very badly want to do something it becomes kind of easy.'

'It's still a long way,' said Fiona. 'And look at what happened to your jeans while you were travelling. I could ask Granny to sew them for you if you like.'

At first I didn't understand, but then I looked down at my legs and tried not to laugh.

'Our jeans are meant to be like that,' I said.

'They're called ripped skinnies,' added Beth. 'They're very popular in ... where we come from.'

If Fiona thought we were crazy, she didn't let on.

'Oh, OK,' she said. 'Sorry if that sounded rude.

Anyway, what are you supposed to do when you get here after your long walk?

I was glad she hadn't asked the hard question about where we'd stayed for the past few nights. I'd been practising a story about a lost tent, but it was totally pathetic.

'We don't have to do anything special here,' I said. 'Just getting here was the challenge. But now we're kind of tired, so, maybe we could rest here for a bit?'

'Of course,' said Fiona. 'Stay as long as you like. While you're here, Granny won't try to give me another knitting lesson. Knitting has to be the most boring thing in the whole world.'

'That's what I think too,' said Beth, a bit too enthu-siastically.

I felt sorry for her. It's hard when you meet someone new, and you really, really want to impress them.

It's doubly-hard when the person you're trying to impress is your mother – and she's the same age as you.

'And do you have to walk all the way back home too?' asked Fiona, who didn't seem to notice anything strange about the way Beth was acting. Maybe there were more weirdos around in 1984.

'No,' I said, really quickly before Beth could get any crazy ideas. 'We've got a train ticket from Kilkenny.'

'And how are you going to get to Kilkenny?' This girl sure knew how to ask questions.

'We're not exactly sure yet,' I said. 'Maybe we could—'

But Fiona interrupted me. 'One of our neighbours is in hospital in Kilkenny, and her husband visits her every evening. I know he wouldn't mind giving you a lift.'

'Well, maybe ...' began Beth. 'I'm not sure if ...'

I glared at her. There was no *way* I was going to walk all the way back to Kilkenny. I was *so* over the whole hiking around the country thing.

'We'll take the lift,' I said quickly. 'Thanks very much.'

'He usually goes at about seven,' said Fiona.

'How do you know?' I asked.

Fiona rolled her eyes, looking exactly like Beth. 'Not much happens around here,' she said. 'So I notice his car going past.'

Then she checked her watch – which was giant-sized and made of purple and pink plastic. 'That's nearly five hours away. If you'd like to stay here until then, you'd be very welcome.'

Beth didn't give me a chance to answer. 'We'd love that,' she said. 'Thanks so much.'

Five hours.

Sometimes five hours can be a very long time.

I had a funny feeling this wasn't going to be one of those times.

Chapter Twenty-Three

Fiona threw herself back on the rug, letting her long hair spread around her like a shiny, black halo. She closed her eyes, which made me relax a bit – those pale-blue eyes were much too like Beth's, and they were freaking me out.

At last Beth and I had the chance to look at Fiona properly. She was young and pretty and so ... alive. She looked cool despite her 1980s clothes. They suited her!

I was starting to feel sad again, when Beth jumped up.

'What's to do around here?' she asked.

'Not much,' said Fiona, opening her eyes again. 'Unless ... unless you like swimming.'

'I totally love swimming,' said Beth.

'Totally!' said Fiona, laughing as if she'd never heard the word before.

'Beth's the best swimmer in our whole school,' I said. 'She's got heaps of medals and trophies.'

Fiona grinned at her. 'I love swimming too and ... well I'm not bad at it.'

'Such a strange coincidence,' I said.

Fiona didn't notice my sarcastic tone. 'There's a river just across the next field, and it's safe to swim in. We can go there if you like.'

'But we don't have our swimming things with us,' I said.

Fiona looked at our bags, which we'd flung under a tree. She must have been wondering what we had in them.

What would she say if she knew we were carrying around our schoolbooks and empty lunchboxes and our uniforms?

What would she say if she knew that half the things in our history book hadn't happened yet?

Could she ever understand that our history was her future?

What would she say if she saw my geography homework, most of which I'd copied and pasted from Wikipedia?

I was still staring at my schoolbag when Fiona spoke again. 'You don't have to worry about swimsuits,' she said.

I gasped. Was skinny-dipping a thing in 1984? If it was, I *so* wasn't going to join in.

'My cousins were here last week,' continued Fiona. 'And they left lots of their clothes behind. I can easily find enough swimsuits for the three of us. You wait here, and I'll be as quick as I can.'

I tried not to look too relieved as she ran back into the house.

* * *

'What do you think?' asked Beth.

'I think that this is all so weird, I don't know what to think.'

'No, I mean what do you think of Fiona? Do you like her?'

Suddenly I thought of something terrible.

What if Fiona had turned out to be a complete idiot?

What if she was a creepy mean girl who hurt kittens and picked on weak kids?

What if she was the kind of girl you'd never, ever want to be friends with – even if you were stuck on a desert island with no other company except an ancient, wrinkled turtle and a few squawky parrots?

'Well?' said Beth impatiently.

I smiled at her, glad I was able to tell the truth. 'I think Fiona is absolutely lovely.'

Beth smiled back. 'Thanks,' she said. 'That's what I think too.'

* * *

A few minutes later, Fiona was back with a big gear bag over her shoulder.

'I've told Granny you're here,' she said. 'She phoned our neighbour about getting a lift later, and he said he'll meet you at the end of the road at seven.'

'That's really nice of your granny,' I said.

'She's a sweetie,' said Fiona. 'And she's making us a picnic.'

'OMG,' I said. 'That's so ...'

'OMG?' repeated Fiona. 'What does that mean?'

'It's just a popular saying where we come from,' I said, beginning to understand that they spoke a whole different language back in 1984. 'People say it when they're happy, or surprised or scared, or ... Well, you get the idea – people say it a lot.'

'Strange,' said Fiona. 'Anyway, in this case you should be happy. My granny makes great picnics.'

Of course we were happy.

We were getting food, and we didn't even have to beg for it or steal it.

How brilliant was that?

I thought about telling Fiona how I get hangry

when I haven't eaten, but I couldn't face the explanation that would have to come afterwards, so I just smiled and looked happy.

The side door of the house opened and a woman came out. She was like the granny in a story book – with grey curly hair, rosy cheeks, and a flowery apron dusted with flour.

'My great-grandmother,' breathed Beth.

'Pardon?' said Fiona.

'She just said that she looks like a really great grandmother,' I said quickly.

'So these are your new friends, Fiona,' said her granny. 'It's nice to meet you girls.'

Then she looked at Beth. 'Don't I know you?' she asked.

'Er ... I don't think so,' said Beth.

'But you look very familiar,' said Fiona's granny.

Then I understood what was going on – Fiona's granny was seeing a resemblance between mother and daughter – except that had to be impossible.

'Oh, people are always saying that about Beth,' I

said. 'I guess she's got a common kind of face.'

I don't know if Fiona's granny believed me, but she didn't comment.

'So where have you suddenly appeared from?' she asked.

From the future?

I couldn't tell the truth, and I didn't feel like telling my lie again either. Fiona's granny might ask all the hard questions I had no answers for. So I said nothing.

'Oh, we're just passing through,' said Beth casually.

That seemed to be enough for her great-grandmother.

'Well, it's nice for Fiona to have some young friends to play with,' she said. 'It can't be fun being stuck here with two fuddy-duddies all the time. I hope you all have a lovely swim. Make sure you stay in the safe part of the river, Fiona. Here's your food, and remember not to go in the water straight after eating.'

'We won't,' said Fiona.

She took the basket from her granny and the three of us set off for the river.

Chapter Twenty-Four

It was a perfect golden summer afternoon. We spread out the rug, lay in the sun, and talked. What we said was mostly stupid stuff, but I knew it was exactly the kind of stuff that Beth wanted to hear from this girl who was going to grow up to be her mother.

Fiona told us all about her best friend, Kathleen, and what they liked to do. Their lives sounded pretty much like ours, only with fewer computers and more dodgy pop songs – well, we thought they were dodgy. I guess Fiona would think the same about ours!

'Kathleen and I are going to go to college together,' she said. 'I'm going to be a teacher. I want to teach junior infants, because they're so sweet and funny.'

'OMG,' said Beth suddenly. 'I remember Kathleen. She used to visit Dad and me sometimes but then she and her husband moved to America. She still sends us

a Christmas card every year.'

Fiona was laughing. 'You're so funny,' she said. 'How could Kathleen have a husband? She's only thirteen – and she's not in America, she's gone to Ballybunion with her mum and dad.'

'I think Beth might be thinking of a different Kathleen,' I said, trying to kick my friend without Fiona seeing.

But Fiona was still laughing and I didn't want Beth to feel offended, so I changed the subject back to Fiona's future career.

'So you want to be a teacher?' I asked.

'Definitely,' said Fiona. 'It's my dream.'

I looked at Beth, who nodded to let me know that that plan had worked out for Fiona.

'And I'd like to get married,' continued Fiona. 'And have a baby, well babies really, but just one to start with. And I might give up work for a year or two, because I'd like to stay home and mind my baby. And then maybe I'll set up a playschool and …'

I couldn't bear to hear any more. How could I listen to Fiona's dreams for the future, when I knew for sure they were all going to come to a sudden, sad end?

'Tell me, Fiona,' I interrupted her, 'what's your favourite colour?'

'That's a funny question,' said Fiona.

I know it's a strange question, but I'm under pressure.

I'm desperate to make you stop dreaming dreams that I know are never going to come true.

'It's not that strange a question really,' said Beth, giving me a grateful look. 'Molly and I think you can tell a lot about people by hearing what their favourite colour is.'

Fiona seemed to believe her. She picked a blade of grass and held it up to the light. 'My favourite colour is this exact shade of green.'

'Green is OK, I guess,' said Beth. 'But purple's my favourite. Let's do our favourites of everything. You go first, Fiona. What's your favourite food?'

'Angel Delight.'

'I haven't the faintest idea what that even is,' I said. 'But it sounds totally delicious.'

Beth continued her questions. Very few of the answers made sense to me, but that probably didn't matter. None of this was about me. Beth is brilliant at remembering stuff and I could see that she was filing all the information away, so she could take it out and enjoy it later. She was making herself a virtual memory box.

'Favourite song?' she asked.

'"Girls Just Want To Have Fun" or ... no ... "Time after Time" – one of those two! Definitely something by Cyndi Lauper.'

'Favourite movie?'

'*Curse of the Pink Panther*.'

'Favourite book?'

'*Little Women*.'

Beth stopped her questions abruptly, and I knew exactly why.

'That's my favourite book too,' she whispered, with

tears in her eyes. 'I think my mum might have called me after one of the characters. I wonder if ...'

Things were getting out of hand, and I knew I had to step in.

'My favourite book is *Harry Potter and the Prisoner of Azkaban*,' I said.

'What's it about?' asked Fiona. 'I've never heard of it before.'

'You mean you've never heard of ...?' And then I remembered. 'Oh, it's quite new,' I added quickly. 'It's about this boy called Harry Potter and he thinks he's a normal kid, but he's really a wizard. He goes to this school called Hogwarts, and he's really like a super-hero in the wizard world.'

'I don't mean to offend you,' said Fiona, 'but it doesn't sound all that interesting. I can't see it becoming very popular. None of the kids I know would be interested in reading about wizards.'

How could I even begin to explain?

'Time for a swim,' I said brightly. 'Last one in's a

rotten egg.'

We flung on the old-fashioned bikinis that Fiona gave us, and we leapt into the river splashing and screaming. Even though I was really enjoying myself, after a while, I pretended to be tired. I sat on the bank and watched Beth and Fiona becoming friends. They practised different strokes, and had races, and then they floated on their backs and chatted. They looked great together – a perfect match.

* * *

Later, Fiona unpacked all kinds of wonderful foods from the basket her granny had packed for us. I ate like I hadn't seen food for months, but Beth just picked at stuff, like she didn't care if she ate or not. Beth totally loves food, and that's when I really began to understand how special this afternoon was for her.

When we'd all finished eating, I leaned against a tree and watched my friend closely. Sometimes she

laughed, but sometimes she looked sadder than I had ever seen her before. I wanted to go over and hug her and tell her everything was going to be OK, but I didn't. There would be time for hugs later. For now, all I could do was watch.

After a bit we dressed ourselves and Fiona pulled a hairbrush from her bag and brushed her hair. When she was finished she held the brush towards us.

'Anyone want to use this?'

Beth hesitated. 'My hair gets really tangly when it's wet, so would you mind ...?'

Fiona grinned. 'I love brushing other people's hair. I always do Kathleen's for her. Move over here and I'll do yours.'

Suddenly I thought of all the times my mum had offered to brush Beth's hair for her, and all the times Beth had said no. Maybe she'd always been holding out for this special moment.

I could hardly bear to look as Beth leaned up against Fiona's crossed legs, and Fiona ever-so-gently combed

the tangles from Beth's hair. She continued brushing long after the last tangles had gone, while Beth sat there with her eyes closed and a small sad-sweet smile on her face.

When Fiona finally put down the brush, Beth looked like she was going to cry. I could feel tears coming to my eyes too. There's always a row when my mum brushes my hair – I say she's being too rough, and she says it's my fault for pulling away. I never stopped to think how lucky I was to have her there to fight with.

'Do you want me to brush your hair too, Molly?' asked Fiona.

I shook my head. 'That's OK, thanks. I'm good.'

Fiona made a face. 'I don't mean to insult you or anything,' she said, 'but are you sure you two are from Dublin?'

'Of course we are,' I said, crossing my fingers behind my back. 'Why do you ask?'

'Oh, this probably seems silly, but sometimes you sound more like you've come from America.'

I giggled. My mum is always saying stuff like that – she says it's because we watch too much TV. Now it was funny to hear Beth's mum saying the same thing.

Before I could answer, Beth stood up. 'Do you two mind if I go for a short walk on my own?' she asked. 'I just need to ...'

She didn't finish, but I knew exactly what was going on. Beth was being incredibly brave, but still she needed some time to sort through all the weird stuff that had to be rattling around her brain.

When Beth had gone, I looked at Fiona, wondering what to say. Should I try to explain why my friend always seemed to be running off into the woods? But Fiona smiled at me, and I knew that I didn't have to say anything at all.

I lay face-down beside the river, and dangled my fingers in the cool green water. It was a strange feeling, thinking that this same river was going to keep on flowing until Beth and I got to be born, until we grew up, until our children were old, and even after that.

Maybe sometime I could bring Beth back here, and she could remember this day, and be happy.

Then I sat up quickly. I'd just had the most incredible idea.

'Fiona,' I said. 'I need to ask you a favour – a very, very big favour.'

'Of course,' she said. 'Just ask.'

'It's a bit complicated,' I said. 'I need you to do something, and it's really, really important, even though I can't explain exactly why.'

'Can I ask you questions?'

'Sure you can – but I probably won't be able to answer them. You'll just have to trust me.'

Fiona sat up. 'You've got me interested now. Tell me what you want me to do.'

'Thanks,' I said. 'You see it's Beth's birthday in a few days' time, and ...'

Chapter Twenty-Five

When Beth came back I was dozing on the rug. I opened one eye to see her standing over me, with her phone in her hand.

I felt like thumping her.

Was she trying to freak Fiona out?

'Er ... Beth ...' I began.

'What's that?' asked Fiona, before I could finish.

'It's my mo— I mean, my camera,' said Beth quickly.

Fiona looked at it. 'That's the funniest camera I've ever seen,' she said. 'It's so small. How do you fit the film inside? And what are all those numbers for?'

I felt angry. Was Beth going to spoil everything?

But just as quickly I felt sorry, because I knew exactly where this was leading.

'She's not sure what those numbers are for yet, are you, Beth?' I said. 'You see it's a new ph— I mean a

new camera.'

Beth smiled at me gratefully. 'That's it,' she said. 'I just got it last week and I haven't quite figured it out yet. Do you mind if we try to take a selfie?'

'Selfie?' asked Fiona.

I sighed, and repeated the phrase for the hundredth time – 'That's a thing, back where we come from.'

'Actually,' said Beth, 'I've changed my mind about the selfie. Will you take a picture of Fiona and me, Molly?'

I really, really wanted to argue, but I couldn't.

The girls sat together and I clicked the button.

'Wow,' said Fiona, as we showed her the picture on the screen. 'That's the best camera I've ever seen. It's like magic – but how do you get the picture out to stick in an album?'

'That bit's kind of hard to describe,' I said, too tired to start explaining about computers and printers and USB cables.

'I'll work it out somehow,' said Fiona. 'I'm going to

ask for a camera just like that for my birthday.'

'On the 11th of August,' said Beth.

'How did you know when my birthday was?' asked Fiona, looking puzzled.

'Er ... lucky guess,' said Beth.

That would have been the luckiest guess in the history of the world, but Fiona didn't seem to notice.

'Are those cameras expensive?' she asked. 'Where did you buy it?'

'Er, I don't know if they're available in this country,' said Beth. 'My uncle sent this one from America.'

'My dad's got a cousin in America,' said Fiona. 'Maybe he could pick one up for me. What exactly is it called?'

Beth looked at me desperately. I knew she wanted me to step in and come up with clever answers to all of Fiona's questions.

I couldn't say anything though. I still had Beth's phone in my hand, and I stared at the picture of the two girls. They were smiling. Their hair was blowing in

the wind. And their identical, laughing blue eyes were making me feel so sad I could hardly breathe.

* * *

After a while, Beth took her phone and put it back in her pocket.

I was trying not to cry, and not being very successful. I rubbed my eyes, pretending that I'd got dust in them.

'Tell Fiona one of your jokes,' I said to Beth, desperate for something to distract me.

'Sure,' said Beth. 'What's brown and sticky? A stick.'

She told about twenty jokes in a row, and then Fiona told some too. It was strange how many of our jokes that Fiona knew already – and how many of Fiona's had survived for us.

'Your turn, Molly,' said Fiona then.

I've never been very good at telling jokes, and now I couldn't think of a single one. The two girls were star-

ing at me though, and I felt bad. Then I remembered one.

'Oh, OK, I said. 'I've thought of one. Dad told it to me the last time we Skyp— I mean talked on the phone. This is it – *What did the spider do on the computer? Made a website.*'

Beth rolled her eyes. 'That's so lame,' she said.

'I don't get it either,' said Fiona. 'What's a website?'

I tried to explain what a website was but Fiona looked at me like I was speaking a foreign language.

'Sorry, Fiona,' I said in the end. 'Beth's right. It was a rubbish joke.'

So Beth told a good old fashioned knock-knock joke and the three of us laughed a bit too enthusiastically.

* * *

The sun began to sink behind the trees, and it was getting cold.

'I need to get back,' said Fiona. 'Granny worries if I stay out too late, and you'll have to leave for Kilkenny soon.'

We gathered up the stuff and walked slowly back to the gate of Fiona's granny's house. We stood there for a minute, embarrassed.

At last Fiona broke the silence. 'I really enjoyed spending time with you two today,' she said. 'It's a pity you've got to go back home.'

'Maybe we don't have to go,' said Beth.

'But—' I began.

'Don't we get extra girl guide points if we stay for the night?' asked Beth, smiling at me sweetly. 'We might get a gold medal instead of a silver one. And if we stay, we could spend tomorrow with Fiona too.'

Tomorrow.

I hadn't thought about tomorrow. The past days had all been about getting here and meeting Fiona, and I had no idea what was supposed to happen next.

All I could think of were problems.

Where were we supposed to sleep that night?

What were we going to eat? (Even though Fiona's granny's picnic had been delicious, I was starting to feel hungry again.)

And then there was the bigger problem. We couldn't stay there forever, so was it best to leave now, before things got even more complicated, before Fiona started to ask impossible questions that would spoil everything?

Beth was staring at me, silently begging me to help her. It was the hardest thing I'd ever done, but I knew I had to be tough.

'We've got to go, Beth,' I said. 'Fiona's neighbour will be leaving for Kilkenny soon. And Mum is meeting us off the train, remember? If we're not there she'll go crazy. We'd love to stay longer, Fiona, but we can't. We really can't.'

Fiona looked disappointed.

I glanced at Beth. Her face was white, and her eyes had filled with tears. I put my arm around her, but

she pulled away and took a step closer to Fiona. That's exactly what I'd have done. Sometimes, when I'm really upset, only a hug from my mum helps.

'I wish we could spend more time here,' said Beth. '... but Molly's right, ... we've got to go now ... I'd love to come back some day, but I'm not sure if that's ever going to happen ... we had a really, really great time, though ... and ... please, Fiona remember this ... when you're older ... be careful on the stairs ... always hold on to the banisters ... terrible things happen some-times ... you could ... just be careful ... always be careful on the stairs ...'

She stopped talking and began to sob.

Beth and I had spent a lot of time talking about whether you can change something that has already happened. I still hadn't made up my mind – but I couldn't blame Beth for trying.

Could Beth's warning really stop her mum from falling down the stairs?

Could she change things so her mum wouldn't die?

Could Beth fix it so she could live happily ever after with her mum and her dad and a houseful of younger brothers and sisters?

And even if that was the thing Beth wanted most in the whole world, was it right?

Was it the way things were meant to be?

The whole thing was *way* too complicated for me, and even thinking about it made my head hurt.

'We have to go, Beth,' I said, putting my arm around her again. 'Bye, Fiona. It's been really nice spending time with you. Thanks for the picnic, and the loan of the swimming stuff, and ... everything.'

I heard the sound of a car engine at the end of the road, and then a quick beep-beep.

Beth moved away from me and wiped tears from her eyes. 'I've figured out that you don't hug a whole lot nowadays ... er ... I mean around this part of the country,' she said to Fiona. 'And I don't want you to think I'm weird or anything, but could you break the rules ... for me ... because ... well because I'm upset?'

She reached out her arms, and Fiona stepped forwards and hugged her tightly. I put my head down and tried not to cry.

At last Beth pulled free. 'Thank you, Fiona,' she whispered. 'You'll never know how much that means to me.'

'That's OK,' said Fiona. 'Well ... maybe I'll see you around some time.'

'I'd love that so much,' said Beth. 'I'd really, really love that.'

And then Fiona watched as Beth and I walked slowly away from her.

We'd almost got to the bend in the lane, when Beth stopped.

'I've got to go back,' she said.

'But—'

'I'll only be one second, I promise.'

Before I could argue any more, she turned and ran back towards Fiona.

While I was still trying to figure out what to do,

Beth was back beside me. Her eyes were still red, but she looked happier.

'What happened?' I asked. 'Why did you need to go back?'

Beth grinned. 'I didn't want to leave on a sad note – I couldn't have Fiona thinking I was some loser weirdo, so I decided to tell her one more joke.'

'Did she get it?'

Beth shrugged. 'I don't know, but she laughed anyway, and that's what counts. I'm glad I made her laugh.'

Chapter Twenty-Six

Fiona's neighbour was a kind man who talked a lot about cows and pigs and stuff. By the time he dropped us at the station in Kilkenny, I felt ready to do a degree in agricultural science. (And I probably smelled like I'd been rolling around in pig poo.)

'Thanks so much,' we called as we climbed out of the car.

'You're very welcome,' he said. 'And if you ever need another lift, just let me know.'

'We will,' I said, feeling guilty at how much I hoped we'd never, ever be back there again.

It was only as we headed up the steps to the station that I realised how tense and nervous I'd been for the past few hours. Of course I wanted Beth to be happy, but what if hanging out with her mum made her sadder than she had been before?

What if I'd stood by and watched while she did something really, really stupid?

Beth was looking at her phone. She moved on from the picture of her and Fiona, and started to set up the 'electronic booking system'.

'Let's hope your battery doesn't die,' I said.

'I think it's OK. I've got 5 per cent left – but let's hope our clever trick works again.'

The ticket-checker was a young, cute guy wearing a suit that was much too big for him.

Beth smiled and held out her phone with the message on the screen. The ticket-checker scratched his head. 'What's all this about?'

'It's the new electronic booking system,' I said.

He took the phone from Beth's hand and turned it over and over like it was the most amazing thing he'd ever seen. I wondered if he'd remember this moment in future years, when he got his own phone.

I wondered if he could imagine a future where only a total loser would go out without one of these

in their pocket.

'Well, I've seen everything now,' he said, as he very carefully handed the phone back to Beth. 'Just wait till I tell my friends about this. I bet they won't even believe me.'

'People can be very old-fashioned,' I said.

'Not me,' he said proudly. Then he pulled up his sleeve and showed us a clunky plastic watch that looked like it belonged in a museum.

'Er ... that's very interesting,' I said, because he seemed to be waiting for us to be impressed.

'And it's got a calculator and everything. I saw it on *Tomorrow's World*.'

'*Tomorrow's World*?' asked Beth.

He looked at her like she was an idiot. 'You know, *Tomorrow's World* – the best TV programme on the planet? You wouldn't believe some of the fancy futuristic stuff they have on it.'

I smiled to myself. Did he know that to us, this was yesterday's world?

Could he ever understand that Beth and I lived in a world where watches have phones and cameras and things to count your footsteps and measure your heartbeat and ...

He patted the watch like it was the most precious thing in the universe, and then he smiled at us. 'Have a safe journey.'

And that's exactly what we did.

* * *

It was dark when we finally got back to the shopping centre. I felt tired, like I'd run a couple of marathons or climbed a few mountains or something.

'The whole place is locked up,' said Beth. 'What are we going to do now?'

I was all out of ideas, so we stood there for a long time, doing nothing. Finally, a small door near us opened up, and two women in uniforms came out. They walked away, and I raced over to grab the door

before it slammed shut.

'We're in,' I whispered.

Even though there were lots of lights on, the shopping centre was empty and kind of creepy. I missed the weirdly dressed shoppers and the jingly-jangly music – I'd got kind of used to it. Once or twice we heard footsteps, and we had to duck behind some plastic plants, but we didn't see anyone.

Finally we turned the last corner.

'OMG,' I said.

The pink squashy couches were there. The jungly plants were there. And also there was a small grey coloured door, with a sign on it – *Rico's Store. Emergency Entrance.*

'That's totally weird,' said Beth. 'How come we couldn't see that door the last time we were here? And what's an emergency ENTRANCE?'

'Don't know and don't care,' I said, as I grabbed her hand and ran towards the door. 'I've had enough of 1984. I want to go home.'

I pulled the door open, and without saying anything, the two of us raced inside, and the door closed silently behind us.

We were back in the strange, dark, cinnamon-scented place. This time I was in too much of a hurry to feel properly scared. I ran towards the light, pulling Beth behind me.

'Oh,' I said.

Rico was standing exactly where we had left him, still polishing the sparkly blue glass bottle. He didn't seem the tiniest bit surprised to see us.

'You're back already,' he said. 'Did you find what you were looking for?'

'We totally did,' said Beth. 'Thank you.'

He smiled and returned to his glass-polishing. I didn't fancy hanging around making small talk, so I rushed past the man, and out the front door of the shop. Beth followed me, and we stood together in the smelly alleyway.

Beth rubbed her eyes. 'I know this is going to sound

crazy,' she said. 'But I think I've just had the most vivid dream of my entire life. It was 1984, and there was bad music and big hair and we walked for miles and miles and ... I met my mum and ... we hung out together ... and it was amazing ... and ... it seems so real ... so how could it be a dream?'

I hugged her. 'It sounds like a dream,' I said, 'except that I had the exact same one.'

'You did?'

'Yeah, and ...'

Then I heard a familiar voice coming from the end of the alleyway. It was my mum – without the tantrum and the frizzy hair and the weird yellow dungarees. Now she was all grown up, the way she was supposed to be.

Mum was saying goodbye to Dora, who was picking up her shopping bags. They kissed the air next to each other's cheeks and then they both walked away.

'I know you said that woman can talk forever,' said Beth, 'but this is ridiculous.'

She was right.

How long had Mum and Dora been talking?

How long had Beth and I been gone?

I turned to look at Beth. Her face had gone pale, and she didn't seem to care about Mum and Dora any more.

'Two per cent of battery,' she said as she pulled her phone out of her pocket. 'That should be enough.'

Her hand was shaking so much, she accidentally skipped back to her oldest photographs. She held the phone between us as she scrolled forwards.

I saw the pictures of Beth and me hanging ornaments on our Chrismas tree.

I saw the two of us cracking open a huge Easter egg.

I saw us messing in the garden.

I saw the funny pictures we'd taken a week earlier when we were getting ready to go to the cinema.

And then ...

'No!' said Beth. 'That can't be right. It just can't be.'

She had stopped at the most recent photograph,

the one I'd taken in 1984 – but the two smiling girls had vanished. The picture was grey and cloudy, like someone had covered it with smoke. In the middle of the screen were two fuzzy shapes that could have been anyone – or anything.

I hugged her. 'I'm so sorry, Beth,' I said.

'But it shouldn't be like that. You showed me the picture. I saw it. She saw it. We both looked really nice. It was perfect. What happened?'

'I'm not sure, but I guess photos don't time-travel as easily as people do?'

'It's OK,' she said, but I knew it wasn't.

How could it possibly be OK?

In the distance, I could hear the sound of a guitar being tuned, and some drums. There was lots of clapping and a huge cheer.

'We can still get to the concert on time,' I said. 'All we have to do is ...'

'No,' said Beth. 'If you don't mind, I'd prefer to go home. I'll text Lucy and tell her that ... I'll tell her that

time ran away with us.'

She gave a big yawn, and I remembered how tired I was.

'Sure,' I said. 'Let's go home. Feels like I haven't been there for years.'

* * *

By the time we got home, Mum was in the kitchen, making pizza. Beth's dad's jacket was thrown over a chair, and Beth's trainers were in the corner. And then I understood – nothing had changed while Beth and I were wandering around the country in 1984. It was as if we'd never gone anywhere. Jim and Beth still lived here, and despite Beth's warning, her mum was still dead.

'You're home early,' said Mum.

'Oh,' I said quickly. 'The debating blitz was cancelled.'

'That's a pity,' said Mum. 'Anyone hungry?' – like

Beth and I ever answered 'no' to that question.

'We're starving,' said Beth and I together, as we sat down.

I gazed around the kitchen, like I'd never seen it before. I touched the table and was surprised to feel the familiar smooth wood under my fingers. Everything felt shaky and strange, like nothing was right, or real.

When Mum came over and put plates on the table, I looked at her like she was a stranger.

'What?' she asked, when she noticed how I was staring at her. 'Have I got flour on my face?'

'No, Mum. It's not that. You look lovely.'

It's just that, a few minutes ago you were a sulky teenager, and I can't figure out how you turned into my mum.

Do you remember that once in 1984 two weirdos showed up at your place looking for an imaginary puppy?

Do you have any idea what just happened?

But Mum had already turned back to the cooker, and the moment was gone.

Beth and I each ate a ton of pizza, and then we helped Mum to tidy the kitchen.

Just as we finished, Beth's dad came in. Beth raced over and hugged him for ages and ages. When she finally let him go, he laughed.

'That's a nice welcome,' he said. 'But you'd think you hadn't seen me for years.'

'I feel like I haven't,' said Beth, brushing her hair away from her face.

Jim went pale. 'Do that again, Beth,' he said.

'What? This?' asked Beth, doing the same thing again. Suddenly I realised where I'd seen that exact same gesture before.

Jim gave a nervous laugh. 'That's so strange,' he said. 'For a moment there, you looked uncannily like your mother.'

Mum put her hand on Beth's shoulder. 'Then her mother must have been very, very beautiful,' she said.

'She was,' whispered Beth. 'She totally was.'

* * *

Jim went upstairs to change out of his work clothes.

'I'm going to get started on my homework,' said Beth. 'I'll be in my room if anyone wants me.'

I followed her into the hall.

'You OK?' I asked.

'I'm not sure. I think so. I just need to sleep for a while. I need to sleep for about twenty years.'

'What's with you two girls today?' said Mum when I went back into the kitchen. 'You hardly said a word while you were eating your pizza. Why are you so quiet all of a sudden?'

Because we're jetlagged and shell-shocked?

Because a few minutes ago we were back in 1984 and it's hard to readjust?

Mum came over and put her arms around me. I cuddled against her, suddenly realising how lucky I was to have her in my life.

'You're sure there's nothing you want to tell me?' she asked, stroking my hair.

There was lots I wanted to tell her, but I didn't know where to begin. It was all far too crazy and impossible.

'We're just tired,' I said, pulling away from her.

Too late, I realised that was the wrong thing to say.

'That's because you stayed up too late last night. You girls think you know everything. You ...'

That reminded me. 'Mum, remember how you told me that you never shouted at your mother when you were young?'

'Yes.'

'Well, was that really true?'

I wasn't quite sure where this conversation was going. If Mum continued to deny it, how was I going to prove her wrong?

But Mum sat down at the kitchen table. 'Know what, Molly? I've been thinking about that during the day – and maybe I didn't tell you the whole truth. My mother expected respect, just like I do, but ... well,

teenagers will be teenagers, and I probably had my moments.'

I grinned. I knew that this was as much of an apology as I was going to get. I put my hand in my pocket. 'I have a surprise for you, Mum. Close your eyes,' I instructed, as I pulled out the sample of Smitty. Mum obeyed. 'Now hold out your hand.'

'Is this going to hurt?' she asked.

I didn't answer. I pulled the stopper from the tiny glass bottle and dabbed a drop of the liquid onto Mum's wrist. Then I lifted her wrist and held it towards her nose.

'Smell.'

Mum inhaled and a slow smile spread over her face.

'Smitty,' she whispered. 'I smell Smitty.'

Much later she opened her eyes.

'Wow,' she said. 'That was like going back in time.' Mum took the package from my hand. She examined the white wrapping with red spot. 'Where on earth did you get this?' she asked.

'On eBay,' I said, hoping she wouldn't stop to think about how long it takes to bid and negotiate and post.

Mum sniffed her wrist again.

'For a minute there, I was a frizzy-haired, dungaree-wearing teenager again – but you probably can't imagine that.'

'You'd be surprised, Mum,' I said, grinning. 'You'd be surprised.'

Chapter Twenty-Seven

The next few days were very weird. When I woke up in the mornings, I was never sure if it was the present or the past. I had really vivid dreams, and they got all mixed up with reality. I felt like my brain was all scrambled up and needed to settle down again.

* * *

I went into Beth's room early on the morning of her birthday. I gave her the top and the bracelet that Mum had helped me pick out, and she showed me the super-cool jacket her dad had bought for her.

I couldn't concentrate though. I felt nervous. Maybe what I was about to do was very wrong.

Things had been a bit weird between Beth and me since our trip to the past. I often mentioned it,

but Beth never wanted to talk about it – not properly. She'd laugh about the clothes and the hairstyles, but any time I mentioned her mum, she'd start to talk about something else.

In the end I took a deep breath. If I didn't do this now, there was a real danger I was never going to do it.

'I've got another present for you, Beth,' I said.

'But the top and the bracelet are enough. They're both lovely and ...'

'It's not that kind of present. It's something very different.'

I reached into my pocket, pulled out a piece of paper, and handed it to her.

'I didn't read it,' I said.

This was true, but once or twice I'd had to sit on my hands to stop myself.

Once I even half-unfolded it before I found the strength to shove it back into my pocket.

'I'm sorry it's so crumpled,' I said. 'I didn't want you to know that I had it, so I had to carry it in my shoe

for a while.'

Beth stared at the piece of paper, but didn't move.

'Take it,' I said, feeling like the wicked queen giving Snow White the poisoned apple.

Was this a huge, stupid mistake?

Very slowly, Beth took the paper from my hand and unfolded it.

'It's a timetable – for buses from Kilkenny to Carlow. That *so* isn't funny, Molly.'

I grabbed the paper, turned it over and handed it back to her. 'This side,' I said.

Beth began to read, but after a second, she dropped the paper onto the bed between us.

'I can't do this,' she said. 'It's too hard.'

I held her hand and we sat there for ages. The paper had landed upside down, so I passed the time by learning that in 1984 the buses ran from Carlow to Kilkenny every hour, and that the fare was 75 pence.

'Could you …?' began Beth.

I was glad when she stopped.

I soooo didn't want to hear the end of her sentence.

I soooo didn't want to read the letter.

What if it was awful?

What if it made Beth even more upset than she had been before?

But then I realised that wasn't fair.

I was the one who had asked Fiona to write the letter, and once it was written, there was no unwriting it. I had to take responsibility.

'Would you like me to read it to you?' I asked.

Beth nodded.

I settled myself on Beth's pillows. She lay across my legs and closed her eyes.

I picked up the paper. The handwriting was tiny and neat. I took a deep breath and began to read.

Dear Beth,

Molly has asked me to write you a note. She didn't explain why, but it seems important, and she said it would mean a lot to you, so .. here goes.

I hope you have a lovely thirteenth birthday. I'm sorry you'll be so far away and I won't be there to give you a present. I know I've just met you, but in a funny way, I feel as if I've known you for ages. I wish you lived near me, or went to my school, because I think we could be friends. (But Molly's really nice — you're lucky to have a friend like her.)

I've never known anyone whose mum has died, so I don't know what to say next. I'm even a bit embarrassed — which I know is stupid. You must be feeling very sad because your mum isn't there with you on your special day. On my birthday, my mum gives me a kiss for every year. It's a bit crazy (especially now that I'm older, and there are so many kisses), but I sort of like it too. I bet your mum wishes she was with you today — I think she would be very proud.

Love from Fiona

I stopped reading then, and put the paper down.

'She finishes with thirteen x's,' I said.

Beth opened her eyes. She picked up the paper and ran her finger along the lines of writing.

'My mum touched this,' she said. 'She wrote it specially for me.'

She folded the paper carefully, and slipped it into her pocket.

'Thank you, Molly,' she whispered. 'That's the best birthday present I've ever, ever got.'

'So you're not upset?'

'No. Before we did all this crazy time-travelling thing, I didn't have a mum, and I still don't, so nothing has changed. But somehow ... everything has changed.'

'I'm not sure I understand.'

'I've met her. I've spoken to her. She laughed at my jokes. I laughed at her jokes – and some of them sooo weren't funny. I told her about my dream of being a software developer. She had no idea what that even was, but I'm glad I told her anyway. She brushed my hair. She even told me what her favour-

ite colour is.'

'And you're sure that doesn't make it harder?'

She shook her head. 'Like I told you before, not knowing was always the worst part. And the more questions I asked about my mum, the less I seemed to know. It was like I ended up with a huge box of pieces from different jigsaw puzzles – pieces that were never, ever going to fit together. And now ... well, when you're missing someone, it's a help to know who exactly it is that you're missing.'

I smiled. 'I'm really glad,' I said.

'Thanks, Molly.'

She hugged me for a long time.

'So what do you want to do today?' I asked. 'It's your birthday, so you can decide.'

Beth thought for a minute.

'We could go back to Rico's Store,' she said. 'Maybe we should get to know our teenaged dads?'

I shook my head. 'No way. I've had enough time–travelling for this week. How about we go to the

pictures? My treat.'

And so my best friend and I set off for a perfect, normal day.

www.obrien.ie